In Our Nature

A MELANIE KROUPA BOOK

In Our Nature

STORIES OF WILDNESS

Selected and introduced by
Donna Seaman

DORLING KINDERSLEY PUBLISHING, INC.

A Melanie Kroupa Book

Dorling Kindersley Publishing, Inc., 95 Madison Avenue, New York, New York 10016

Visit us on the World Wide Web at http://www.dk.com

Dorling Kindersley books are available at special discounts for bulk purchases for sales promotions or premiums. Special editions, including personalized covers, excerpts of existing guides, and corporate imprints can be created in large quantities for specific needs. For more information, contact Special Markets Dept., Dorling Kindersley Publishing, Inc., 95 Madison Ave., New York, NY 10016; fax: (800) 600-9098.

Library of Congress Cataloging-in-Publication Data
In our nature : stories of wilderness / selected and introduced by Donna Seaman.
p. cm.
Contents: Swamp boy / Rick Bass — Barred owl / Chris Offutt — Amen / Linda Hogan — My life as a bat / Margaret Atwood — Erzulie / Pauline Melville — The open lot / Barry Lopez — Everything is about animals / Francine Prose — Willi / E.L. Doctorow — Wolf at the door / Percival Everett — I got a guy once / Tess Gallagher — Four calling birds, three French hens / Lorrie Moore — Men on the moon / Simon J. Ortiz — Weeds / Rick DeMarinis — The heart of the sky / Kent Meyers.
ISBN 0-7894-2642-0
1. Nature stories, American.   2. Human-animal relationships—Fiction.   3. Wilderness areas—Fiction.   4. Animals—Fiction.   I. Seaman, Donna.
PS648.N32 I5 2000   813'.010836—dc21   00-029475

Book design by Jennifer Browne.
The text of this book is set in 12 point Stempel Garamond.

Printed and bound in U.S.A.

First Edition, 2000
2 4 6 8 10 9 7 5 3 1

For my parents,

Elayne and Hal Seaman,

with love

In Wildness is the preservation of the World.
  —Henry David Thoreau, "Walking"

Take earth for your own large room
and the floor of earth
carpeted with sunlight
and hung around with silver wind
for your dancing place
  —May Swenson, "Earth Your Dancing Place"

Yes! No!
The swan, for all his pomp, his robes of glass and petals,
wants only to be allowed to live on the nameless pond. The
catbrier is without fault. The water thrushes, down among
the sloppy rocks, are going crazy with happiness.
Imagination is better than a sharp instrument. To pay
attention, this is our endless and proper work.
  —Mary Oliver, "Yes! No!"

CONTENTS

THE CHARACTER OF NATURE

Nature tells so many stories. What could be more enthralling than the lurid, though luminous, tale of femme fatale fireflies? Or more poignant than hummingbirds dying in their sleep because they live at such a flutter that their rapid hearts cannot manage? The saga of ancient hominids applying raw talents, obsessions, and guts to triumph in a ruinous world remains an epic of startling ingenuity, sorrow, and humor that spans millennia and includes millions of quirky characters.

What should we make of our own nature, our own wildness? We are wonderfully animal in our habits, fears, and family ways. True, we are different from other animals, just as a cougar is different from a giraffe, and how we differ is probably untranslatable because our senses and mental fantasia have evolved to cope with unique threats and enticements. But our instincts? Our motives? Our basic needs?

Pure animal. Watch a bird or squirrel run its errands, and you'll discover all-too-familiar struggles over status, resources, and attachments. Pretending we're a ruling elite isn't good for the planet, but it also isn't good for our own sense of origin, belonging, wholeness, and spirituality. Nature isn't an alien force that combats us; nor does it surround us. We *are* nature, and our cities and inventions, like termite mounds, are part of that complexity.

Impatient by instinct, we use technology to sidestep evolution; instead of waiting for our eyes to evolve, we power them with telescopes, microscopes, and MRIs. The technology we invent to extend our senses may feel other and nonliving, but it's as much a product of our animal nature as is a wombat's burrow. We just don't like to think of it in that way because doing so seems to trivialize us. That's a fundamental problem we have with nature. We believe it is beneath us, or rather behind us. We believe that we are evolution's goal and that animal is dirty, low-class, immoral. We think we can somehow shed our animal nature. We feel valuable only if we can master something, or someone, and unfortunately we like to test that status by regularly proving our dominion. Thus we dam rivers, we level forests, we move mountains, and we hunt animals to extinction.

How we fit into the natural world, what sort of beings we wish to be, and the role we might play in shaping the future of the planet all are questions we'll be forced to consider one day. We may be compassionate beasts, but we're also bullying and destructive. Accepting our own wildness, rejoicing in it, will be an important step toward learning how best to promote what we love about human nature and to curb what shames us. If we can achieve that, a refined sense of ourselves as fundamentally animal, then the world we share—what we call nature—will feel homier, and we'll want to protect it like a second skin.

Often in fiction nature has loomed as a monstrous character, an adversary dishing out retribution for moral slippage, or as a nightmare region of chaos and horror where fanged beasts crouch, ready to attack. But sometimes it beckons as a zone of magic, mysticism, inspiration, and holy conversion. A character usually must choose between worlds, which means choosing between equally important parts of his heritage, and rarely do we find a full integration into the environment on the one hand and into society on the other. Neither choice is bound to satisfy completely.

When humans invent stories, they seize the second hands of all the clocks in the universe, and for golden moments nature becomes a realm they can revise. One of the things I find endearingly strange about human beings is our passion for reforming the world, not just so that we may survive with less toil and insecurity but to reflect our innermost feelings. Imagine that. In the cosmic scheme of things that's a remarkable thing for matter to do. Remarkable for our species, upright apes, whose niche is creativity, but even more remarkable for organisms whose atoms were forged in an early chaos of the sun.

INTRODUCTION BY
DONNA SEAMAN

ON THE EDGE OF WILDERNESS

These are my earliest memories: I'm lying on my back in a crib, looking through its rails. It's daytime, quiet and still. Suddenly the gauzy white fabric on the wall across the room lifts and swells. It seems to be reaching for me; I hold my breath. The room brightens, and a moment later I feel the caress of fresh, fragrant air. Astonishment gives way to bliss.

I also remember crawling on all fours outdoors. I feel the heat of the sun on my back and see my hands push out in front of me and sink into a soft patterned blanket. Intent on motion, I leave its familiar terrain behind, and the prickliness of gleamy green grass sends a shock up my arm when I press my hand into its moist warmth. I absorb the electricity of its aliveness, inhale its sweet but tangy scent, and hesitate, amazed and unsure.

Indelible moments of pure sensuous awareness, these

recollections illuminate the threshold between wilderness and civilization, the place where most of us dwell. We envision our species as elevated above the myriad other beings that sing our planet to life, from the infinity of microorganisms that stoke the fire of creation and the smolder of decay to the great green lungs of the bird-filled rain forests. Bipedal, blessed with opposable thumbs, image-obsessed, language-mad, and self-centered, we ignore the simple truth that prompted the seer Dylan Thomas to write: "The force that through the green fuse drives the flower / Drives my green age...." Again and again we must be reminded by poets, fiction writers, and naturalists that the life force that causes plants to bloom and makes the eyes of animals glisten is the very same vitality that charges our minds and sustains our souls.

In spite of our machines, our plastics, and our artificial ingredients, we are as much a part of nature as any other animal. The wildness of the wolf is the wildness we feel in our blood when we long to cast off the trappings of civilization and simply be alive beneath the starry sky. Enmeshed in the web of life, we identify strongly with our fellow creatures both domestic and wild. We are devoted to the tending of plants, and we are profoundly affected by the beauty of a sunset, the curl of a breaking wave, the splendor of trees in autumn, and the immensity of mountains. But it is also in our nature to be inordinately dazzled by our own inventions and to injure the living things we love.

Our perceptions of nature are rooted in cultural traditions, especially the nearly universal myth of a lost paradise, of a halcyon time when our ancestors lived in perfect harmony with the earth. Certainly our animalness and oneness with nature were more evident when our technologies were simpler and when our numbers were few and our impact on our surroundings was minimal. But our large brains harbor inquisitive and creative minds, and we have not been content with mere survival. After millennia of living in fear of nature's awesome power, our forefathers embarked on what we like to call progress, creating increasingly elaborate defenses against the perilous dark, cold and heat, flood and drought.

Men sought to tame wilderness to satisfy their needs for comfort, safety, and convenience. Successive generations have fine-tuned these requirements, and we continue to progress materially even though it has become clear that we are doing more harm than good to ourselves and our planet. It is this drive to order and change the world that keeps us in perpetual exile from Eden. It is the wildness within us that makes us dream of wilderness and to imagine it as paradise from within our car-studded cities of stone, glass, and steel.

Our longing for wilderness increases in direct proportion to our eradication of it. People who live wholly urbanized lives, spending little time outdoors and rarely stopping to notice life that is not human-made, suffer emotionally and spiritually, cut off, as they are, from our souls' well-spring. We need more than the flat world born of our synthetically directed thoughts—our walls and cubicles, television and computer screens. We need to feed our senses with sunshine and wind, night and rain, hills, trees, and flowing water. We must nurture what master tracker and nature photographer Paul Rezendes calls the "wild within, the larger sense of who we are . . . the whole of the conscious universe."

We hope to experience wildness in our everyday lives or on pilgrimages to such refuges as national parks, but we also find consolation in simply knowing that unspoiled places exist. We look to painting, books, photography, and film for knowledge about natural wonders we may never experience personally. The arts, humanity's flowers, are inextricably rooted in the wild. Our symbols, myths, sacred texts, songs, stories, and poems are as inlaid with nature-based metaphors as a meadow is with wildflowers. And poets and philosophers have been singing nature's praises and warning us of the dire consequences of our cavalier destruction of wilderness for centuries.

Henry David Thoreau wrote his seminal works mere decades before his fellow Americans demonstrated their ability to abruptly obliterate entire animal species, such as the passenger pigeon, demolish such glorious wilderness as the longleaf pine forests of the Southeast, and perpetuate genocide against the people who had thrived on the land's bounty without diminishing it for thousands of years. Long before the advent of electricity and the automobile, inventions that utterly transformed North America, a place as close to paradise as any on earth, Thoreau recognized the wisdom of the American Indian way of life and lamented the development and commercialization of the New England countryside. In his last work, the recently rediscovered *Wild Fruits,* he expresses reverence for lands "as purely primitive and wild as they were a thousand years ago, which have escaped the plow and the axe and the scythe and the cranberry rake, little oases of wildness in the desert of our civilization." He also urgently suggests that places of great natural beauty, even "single ancient trees," should be preserved and reserved permanently for public use.

We have managed to keep our bulldozers and concrete mixers away from some protected places, but wouldn't Thoreau be astounded and appalled at our world? We live within the haze and reek of pollution under the threat of nuclear annihilation in a time of endangered species and decimated forests, prairies, wetlands, rivers, and oceans. Yet human life, with all its joys and sorrows, proceeds much as it always has at its core. A certain amount of obliviousness is in our nature, as are perseverance and our ability to adapt rapidly to even the most aberrant conditions.

The severity of our environmental woes and the need for corrective action are the subject of fierce debate, and the issues involved are complicated and daunting. In the midst of these controversies and conflicts, a sense of moral responsibility and fear of impending disaster have precipitated a renaissance in nature writing. Some of our era's finest literary nonfiction has been written by nature lovers whose ardor is matched by knowledge, intellect, wisdom, and phenomenal powers of observation. We owe a great debt of gratitude to Rachel Carson, Peter Matthiessen, Annie Dillard, Diane Ackerman, Gretel Ehrlich, Terry Tempest Williams, and many others for illuminating our connection to the living world around us and for giving us the concepts and language with which to express our love of wilderness and our concerns about its future as well as our own.

But there are places where even the most supple nonfiction cannot enter, regions of the psyche rife with ambiguity, paradox, and perversity, the deep, shadowy caves and fathomless waters in which we struggle with the conflicting demands of instinct and reason, altruism and greed. These realms are best suited for the unfettered form of fiction. Open-ended, free of factual restraints, and driven by what E. L. Doctorow calls "creative accidents," stories encompass flashes of intuition, the enigmas of dreams, the vagaries of emotion, sheer craziness, impenetrable mystery, and fate's wry blend of coincidence, catastrophe, and inertia.

Gifted and creative nature writers such as Rick Bass and Barry Lopez, two contributors to this short story collection, have turned to fiction to dramatize our species's precarious footing on the threshold between wilderness and civilization, the sacred and the profane, the wondrous and the pragmatic. But most of the fourteen stories gathered together here are written by writers who aren't known for being overtly environmentally oriented. They write about wildness because they write about human nature; one doesn't exist without the other. Their stories, all written within the last two decades, vary in setting, character, and voice, but they share an intensity of feeling and implicit questioning of our perception of ourselves as the planet's dominant species. Their characters both fear and cherish wildness, yet many become aware of their feelings for nature only after witnessing the death of a much-admired animal or suffering the loss of a favorite wild place or a way of life.

Children are exceptionally attuned to both the mysteries of nature and the inexplicability of human behavior. In E. L. Doctorow's shattering tale "Willi," a young boy is enraptured by the "hum of the universe" as he walks through the resplendent meadow behind his family's barn, only to be devastated by the shock of seeing adults transformed into animals in the frenzy of sexual lust. Rick Bass's young hero revels in the secret life of the bayou as he gathers flowers and catches frogs, but he is hounded by a pack of boys who are incensed by his solitary communion with the wild.

Bass's protagonist is one of several characters who are ostracized for their passion for the nonhuman realm. In

Barry Lopez's "The Open Lot," Jane Weddell, a dreamy and intuitive paleontologist, is punished for her lack of professional ambition, then rewarded briefly by a vision of a lost wilderness concealed beneath the veneer of New York City. In "Four Calling Birds, Three French Hens," Lorrie Moore's funny and vibrant heroine is considered odd when she mourns long and hard for her beloved cat.

Misfits and mystics, these characters cross the divide between wilderness and social convention, erring, their peers believe, on the wild side. But characters who try to channel their wildness into civilized pursuits also suffer feelings of alienation and futility. In Francine Prose's "Everything Is About Animals," a biologist who specializes in animal relocation is overcome by grief over the anguish of displaced monkeys. The veterinarian in Percival Everett's elegiac tale is haunted by animals he is unable to save. And the men in Chris Offutt's somber story sicken psychically after leaving their spiritual home, the untamed hills of eastern Kentucky.

Whether it's a wickedly funny story, like Margaret Atwood's "My Life As a Bat" or Simon Ortiz's "Men on the Moon"; or "Weeds," Rick DeMarinis's surreal and disturbing fairy-tale improvisation; Pauline Melville's magical fable "Erzulie"; Tess Gallagher's painfully ironic "I Got a Guy Once"; or the soulful ballad of love regained that Kent Meyers intones in "The Heart of the Sky," these stories embody the dichotomies and confusion of our knotty interpretations of wildness and of ourselves. We are six billion strong and counting. Our voices fill the airwaves, and our footprints, tire tracks, and jet trails mark every vista. Even our love for wilderness is heavy-handed and paradoxical. Hungry for the solace of the wild, we gather in national parks in marauding herds, and as Thoreau observed of our forefathers, "we behave like oxen in a flower garden," trampling delicate plants, forcing animals into exile, polluting the air, making a machine-produced racket, and filling the night sky with star-erasing light.

Sentimental and careless, we seem destined to worship wilderness as we continue to undermine and destroy it. Seekers and praisers of beauty, we find as much cause for rejoicing as for sorrow as we walk the line between what remains of wilderness and our rabidly consumptive civilization. Pattern-focused and word-struck, we love stories—the wild fruits of our imagination—not because they offer solutions to problems but because they illuminate our place in the shimmering universe and open our hearts to the music in our blood—a song beyond measure written in the stars, spun in the seas, and rooted deeply in the teeming earth. Our nature is all nature—wild, mysterious, and full of grace.

In Our Nature

RICK BASS

SWAMP BOY

There was a kid we used to beat up in elementary school. We called him Swamp Boy. I say we, though I never threw any punches myself. And I never kicked him either, or broke his glasses, but I stood around and watched, so it amounted to the same thing. A brown-haired fat boy who wore bright striped shirts. He had no friends.

I was lucky enough to have friends. I was unexceptional. I did not stand out.

We'd spy on Swamp Boy. We'd trail him home from school. Those times we jumped him—or rather, when those other boys jumped him—the first thing they struck was always his horn-rim glasses. I don't know why the thick, foggy-lensed glasses infuriated them so much. Maybe they believed he could see things with them, invisible things that they could not. This possibility, along with some odd chemistry, seemed to drive the boys into a frenzy. We would go after him into the old woods along the bayou that he loved. He went there every day.

We followed him out of school and down the winding clay road. The road led past big pines and oaks, past the puddles of red water and Christ-crown brambles of dewberries, their white blossoms floating above thorns. He'd look back, sensing us I think, but we stayed hidden amid the bushes and trees. His eyesight was poor.

Now and then he stopped to search out blackberries and the red berries that had not yet ripened. His face scrunched up like an owl's when he tasted their tart juices. Like a little bear, he moved on then, singing to himself, taking all the time in the world, plucking the berries gingerly to avoid scratching his plump hands and wrists on the awful tangle of daggers and claws in which the berries rested. Sometimes his hand and arm got caught on the curved hooks of the thorns, and he'd be stuck as though in a trap. He'd wince as he pulled his hand free of the daggers, and as he pulled, other thorns would catch him more firmly; he'd pull harder. Once free, he sucked the blood from his pinprick wounds.

And when he'd had his fill of berries and was nearing the end of the road, he began to pick blossoms, stuffing them like coins into the pockets of his shirt and the baggy shorts he always wore—camper-style shorts with zip-up compartments and all sorts of rings and hooks for hanging compasses and flashlights.

Then he walked down to the big pond we called Hidden Lake, deep in the woods, and sprinkled the white blossoms onto the surface of the muddy water. Frogs would cry out in alarm, leaping from shore's edge with frightened chirps. A breeze would catch the floating petals and carry them across the lake like tiny boats. Swamp Boy would walk up and down the shore, trying to catch those leaping frogs.

Leopard frogs: *Rana utricularia.*

We followed him like jackals, like soul scavengers. We made the charge about once a week: we'd shout and whoop and chase him down like lions on a gazelle, pull that sweet boy down and truss him up with rope and hoist him into a tree. I never touched him. I always held back, only pretending to be in on it. I thought that if I touched him, he would burn my fingers. We knew he was alien, and it terrified us.

With our hearts full of hate, a terrible, frantic, weak, rotting-through-the-planks hate, we—they, the other boys—would leave him hanging there, red-faced and congested, thick-tongued with his upside-down blood, until the sheer wet weight of the sack of blood that was his body allowed him to slip free of the ropes and fall to the ground like a dead animal, like something dripped from a wet limb. But before his weight let him fall free, the remaining flowers he'd gathered fluttered from his pockets like snow.

Some of the boys would pick up a rock or branch and throw it at him as we retreated, and I was sickened by both the sound of the thuds as the rocks struck his thick body and by the hoots of pleasure, the howls of the boys whenever one of their throws found its target. Once they split his skull open, which instantly drenched his hair, and we ran like fiends, believing we had killed him. But he lived, fumbling free of the ropes to make his way home, bloody-faced and red-crusted. Two days after he got stitched up at the hospital, he was back in the woods again, picking berries and blossoms, and even the dumbest of us could see that something within him was getting strong and that something in us was being torn down.

Berry blossoms lined the road along which we walked each afternoon—clumps and piles of flowers, each mound of them indicating where we'd strung him up earlier. I started to feel bad about what I was doing, even though I was never an attacker. I merely ran with the other boys for the spectacle, to observe the dreamy phenomenon of Swamp Boy.

One evening in bed I woke up with a pain in my ribs, as if the rocks had been striking me rather than him, and my mouth tasted like berries, and I was frightened. There was a salty, stinging feeling of thorn scratches across the backs of my hands and forearms. I have neglected to say that we all wore masks as we stalked and chased him, so he was probably never quite sure who we were—he with those thick glasses.

I lay in the darkness and imagined that in my fright my heart would begin beating faster, wildly, but instead it slowed down. I waited what seemed like a full minute for the next beat. It was stronger than my heart had ever beaten before. Not faster, just stronger. It kicked once, as if turning over on itself. The one beat—I could feel this distinctly—sent the pulse of blood all through my body, to the ends of my hands and feet. Then, after what seemed again like a full minute, another beat, one more round of blood, just as strong or stronger. It was as if I had stopped living and breathing, and it was the beat of the earth's heart in my hurt chest. I lay very still, as if pinned to the bed by a magnet.

The next day we only spied on him, and I was glad for that. But even so, I awakened during the night with that pain in my chest again. This time, though, I was able to roll free of the bed. I went to the kitchen for a glass of water, which burned all the way down as I drank it.

I got dressed and went out into the night. Stars shone through the trees as I walked toward the woods that lay between our subdivision and the school, the woods through which Swamp Boy passed each day. Rabbits sat hunched on people's front lawns like concrete ornaments, motionless in the starlight, their eyes glistening. The rabbits seemed convinced that I presented no danger to them, that I was neither owl nor cat. The lawns were wet with dew. Crickets called with a kind of madness, or a kind of peace.

I headed for the woods where we had been so cruel, along the lazy curves of the bayou. The names of the streets in our subdivision were Pine Forest, Cedar Creek, Bayou Glen, and Shady River, and for once, with regard to that kind of thing, the names were accurate. I work in advertising now, at the top of a steel-and-glass skyscraper from which I stare out at the flat gulf coast, listening to the rain, when it comes, slash and beat against the office windows. When the rain gives way to sun, I'm so high up that I can see to the curve of the earth and beyond. When the sun burns the steam off the skin of the earth, it looks as if the whole city is smoldering.

Those woods are long gone now, buried by so many tons of houses and roads and other sheer masses of concrete that what happened there when I was a child might as well have occurred four or five centuries ago, might just as well have been played out by Vikings in horn helmets or red natives in loincloths.

There was a broad band of tallgrass prairie—waist high, bending gently—that I would have to cross to get to the woods. I had seen deer leap from their beds there and sprint away. I could smell the faraway, slightly sweet odor of a skunk that had perhaps been caught by an owl at the edge of the meadow, for there were so many skunks in the meadow, and so many owls back in the woods. I moved across the silver field of grass in starlight and moonlight, like a ship moving across the sea, a small ship with no others out, only night.

Between prairie and woods was a circle of giant ancient

oaks. You could feel magic in this spot, feel it rise from centuries below and brush against your face like the cool air from the bottom of a deep well. This "buffalo ring" was the only evidence that a herd of buffalo had once been held at bay by wolves, as the wolves tried, with snarling feints and lunges, to cut one of the members out of the herd. The buffalo had gathered in a tight circle to make their stand, heads all facing outward; the weaker ones had taken refuge in the center. Over and over, the sun set and the moon glided across the sky as the wolves kept them in this standoff. Heads bowed, horns gleaming, the buffalo trampled the prairie with their hooves, troughed it up with nose-stinging nitrogen piss and shit in their anger and agitation.

Whether the wolves gave up and left, or whether they darted in, grabbed a leg, and pulled out one of the buffalo—no matter, for all that was important to the prairie, there at the edge of the woods along the slow bayou, was what had been left behind. Over the years, squirrels and other animals had carried acorns to this place, burying them in the rich circular heap of shit-compost. The trees, before they were cut down, told this story.

Swamp Boy could feel these things as he moved across the prairie and through the woods, there at the edge of that throbbing, expanding city, Houston. And I could too, as I held my ribs with both arms because of the strange soreness. I began going into the woods every night, as if summoned.

I would walk the road he walked. I would pass beneath the same trees from which we had hung him, the limbs thick and branching parallel over the road: the hanging trees. I would walk past those piles of flower petals and berry blossoms, and shuffle my feet through the dry brown oak leaves. Copperheads slept beneath the leaves, cold and sluggish in the night, and five-lined skinks rattled through brush piles, a sound like pattering rain. Raccoons loped down the road ahead of me, looking back over their shoulders, their black masks smudged across their delicate faces.

I would walk past his lake. The shouting frogs fled at my approach. The water swirled and wriggled with hundreds of thousands of tadpoles—half-formed things that were neither fish nor frog, not yet of this world. As they swirled and wriggled in the moonlight, it looked as if the water were boiling.

I would go past the lake, would follow the thin clay road through the starlit forest to its end, to a bluff high above the bayou, the round side of one of the meandering S-cuts that the bayou had carved. I know some things about the woods even though I lived in the city, have never left this city. I know some things that I learned as a child just by watching and listening—and I could use those things in my advertising, but I don't. They are my secrets. I don't give them away.

I would stand and watch and listen to the bayou as it rolled past, its gentle, lazy current always murmuring, always twenty years behind. Stories from twenty years ago, stories that had happened upstream, were only just now reaching this spot.

Sometimes I feel as if I've become so entombed that I have *become* the giant building in which I work—that it is my shell, my exoskeleton, like the sea shell in which a fiddler crab lives, hauling the stiff burden of it around for the rest of his days. The chitin of things not said, things not done.

I would stand there and hold my hurt ribs, feel the breezes, and look down at the chocolate waters, the star glitter reflecting on the bayou's ripples, and I would feel myself fill slowly and surely with a strength, a giddiness that urged me to *jump, jump, jump.* But I would hold back, and instead would watch the bayou go drifting past, carrying its story twenty more years down the line, and then thirty, heading for the gulf, for the shining waters.

Then I'd walk back home, undress, and crawl back into bed and sleep hard until the thunder rattle of the alarm clock woke me and my parents and my brothers began to move about the house. I'd get up and begin my new day, the real day, and my ribs would be fine.

I had a secret. My heart was wild and did not belong among people.

I did what I could to accommodate this discrepancy.

We continued to follow him, through the woods and beyond. Sometimes we would spy on him at his house early in the evenings. We watched him and his family at the dinner table, watched them say grace, say amen, then eat and talk. It wasn't as if we were homeless or anything—this was back when we all still had both our parents, when almost everyone did—but still, his house was different. The whole house itself seemed to come alive when the family was inside it, seemed to throb with a kind of strength. Were they taking it from us as we watched them? Where did it come from? You could feel it, like the sun's force.

After dinner they gathered around the blue light of the television. Our spying had revealed to us that *Daniel Boone* was Swamp Boy's favorite show. He wore a coonskin cap while he watched it, and his favorite part was the beginning, when Dan'l would throw the tomahawk and split the tree trunk as the credits rolled. This excited him so much each time that he gave a small shout and jumped in the air.

After *Daniel Boone,* it would be time for Swamp Boy's mother and father to repair his glasses, if we'd broken them that day. They'd set the glasses down on a big long desk and glue them, or put screws in them, using all sorts of tape and epoxy sealers, adjusting and readjusting them. Evidently his parents had ordered extra pairs, because we had broken them so often. Swamp Boy stood by patiently while his parents bent and wiggled the earpieces to fit him.

How his parents must have dreaded the approach of three in the afternoon, wondering, as it drew near the time for him to get out of school and begin his woods walk home, whether today would be the day that the cruel boys would attack their son. What joy they felt when he arrived home unscathed, back in the safety of his family.

We grew lean through the spring as we chased him toward the freedom of summer. I was convinced that he was absorbing all of our strength with his goodness, his sweetness. I could barely stand to watch the petals spill from his pockets as we twirled him from the higher and higher limbs, could barely make my legs move as we thundered along behind him, chasing him through the woods.

I avoided getting too close, would not become his friend, for then the other boys would treat me as they treated him.

But I wanted to watch.

In May, when Hidden Lake began to warm up, Swamp Boy would sometimes stop off there to catch things. The water was shallow, only neck deep at the center, full of gars, snakes, fish, turtles, and rich bayou mud at its bottom. It's gone now. The trees finally edged in and spread their roots into that fertile swamp bottom, taking it quickly, and no sooner had the trees claimed the lake than they were in turn leveled to make way for what came next—roads, a subdivision, making ghosts of the forest and the lake.

Swamp Boy kept a vegetable strainer and an empty jar in his lunch box. He set his tape-mended glasses down on a rotting log before opening his lunch box, flipping the clasp on it expertly, like a businessman opening his briefcase. He removed his shoes and socks and wiggled his feet in the mud. When his glasses were off like that, we could creep to within twenty or thirty feet of him.

A ripple blew across the water—a slight mystery in the wind or a subtle swamp movement just beneath the surface. I could feel some essence, a truth, down in the soil beneath my feet—but I'd catch myself before saying to the other boys, "Let's go." Instead of jumping into the water or giving myself up to the search for whatever that living essence was beneath me, I watched.

He crouched down, concentrating, looking out over the lake and those places where the breeze had made a little ring or ripple. Then came the part we were there to see, the part that stunned us: Swamp Boy's great race into the water. Building up a good head of steam, running fast and flat-footed in his bare feet, he charged in and slammed his vegetable strainer down into the reeds and rushes. Just as quickly he was back out, splashing, stumbling, having scooped up a big red wad of mud. He emptied the contents onto the ground. The mud wriggled with life, all the creatures writhing and gasping, terrible creatures with bony spines or webbed feet or pincers or whiskers.

After carefully sorting through the tadpoles—in various stages of development; half frog and half fish, looking human almost, like little round-headed human babies—angry catfish, gasping snapping turtles, leaping newts, and hellbenders, he put the catfish, the tadpoles, and a few other grotesqueries in his jar filled with swamp water, and then picked up all the other wriggling things and threw them back into the lake.

Then he wiped his muddy feet off as best as he could, put his shoes and socks and strainer in his lunch box, and walked the rest of the way home barefoot. From time to time he held the jar up to the sun, to look at his prizes swimming around in that dirty water. The mud around his ankles dried to an elephant-gray cake. We followed him to his house at a distance, as if escorting him.

That incredible force field, a wall of strength, when he disappeared into his house, into the utility room to wash up—the whole house glowed with it, something emanated from it. And once again I could feel things, lives and stories, meaningful things, stirring in the soil beneath my feet.

I continued to walk out to the woods each night, awakening with a pain so severe in my chest and ribs, a pain and a hunger both, that I could barely breathe.

Could I run out and catch a frog or a tadpole, launch myself wild-assed into the muddy water? Could I bring a shovel out to the prairie one night and dig down, deep down, in search of an old buffalo skull that would still smell rank and earthy but gleam white in the moonlight when I pulled it up? If I had intended to do any of those things, if I had dared to—if I had had the strength and the courage—I should have done so then.

In the evenings, after spying on him as he watched TV, we'd go home to our own suppers, then return and look in on him again. We wouldn't devil him, just watch him. We'd line up, a couple of us at each window, and peer in from the darkness like raccoons.

In his room Swamp Boy had six aquariums set beneath neon lights. He kept the other lights turned off, so that all you could see were his catfish and the hellish tadpoles. There were filters and air pumps bubbling away in those aquariums, humming softly. The water was so clear that it must have seemed like heaven to those poor rescued creatures that had been living in a Houston mud hole.

The catfish were pretty, as were even the feather-gilled tadpoles—morpho-frogs whose hind legs trailed uselessly behind them. He went from tank to tank, bending over to examine the creatures with his patched-up glasses that made him look like a little surgeon. He pressed his nose against the glass and stared in wonder, open-mouthed, touching the sides of the aquarium with his fingers while the sleek, wild-whiskered catfish and bulge-bellied tadpoles circled and swarmed in lazy schools, rising and falling as if with purpose. He tried to count his charges. We'd see him point at them with his index finger, saying the words out loud or to himself, softly, "One, two, three, four . . ."

There was a bottle of aspirin on his desk and a heater in each of the tanks, for cold winter nights. Whenever he suspected that a catfish or a tadpole was feeling ill, he'd drop an aspirin in the water. It would make a cloudy trail as it fell.

Sometimes he'd lie in bed with his hands behind his head and watch the fish and tadpoles go around and around in their new home. When the moon was up and the lights were off it looked as though his room were under water—as if *he* were under among the catfish.

God, we were devils. It occurred to a couple of the older boys to see how far he could run. Usually we caught him and strung him up fairly quickly, after only a short chase, but one day we tried to run him to exhaustion, to try and pop his fat, strong heart.

After school we put on wolf masks and made spiked collars by driving nails through leather dog collars, which we fastened around our necks. We spoke to one another in snarling laughs, our voices muffled through the wolf masks.

We started out after him the minute he hit the woods, bending our heads low to the ground and pretending to sniff his scent, howling, trotting along behind him, loping and barking. We chased him through the woods and down along the bayou on the other side of a forested ridge. In his fear he started making sounds like a lost calf. There was cane along the bayou, flood-killed, dry-standing ghost bamboo, and Swamp Boy plowed through that as if going through a dead cornfield, snapping the bamboo in all directions, running as if the forces of hell had opened up.

All we were going to do was throw mud on him, once he got too tired to go any farther. Roll him around in the mud a little, maybe. And break his glasses, of course.

But this time he was really afraid.

It was exciting, chasing him through the tiger-slash stripes of light, following the swath of his flight through all that knocked-over dead bamboo. It was about the most exciting thing we had ever done.

We chased him to the small bluff overlooking the bayou, and Swamp Boy paused for only the briefest of seconds before making a Tarzan dive into the milky brown water. He swam immediately for the slick clay bank on the other side, toward north Houston where the rich people lived, where I imagined he would skulk up to some rich person's backyard, shivering, shoeless, smelling like some vile swamp thing, waiting until dark, so large was his shame. He'd hide in their bushes, perhaps, before creeping up to the back porch—still dripping wet and muddy, and bloody from where the canes had stabbed him—and then, crying, ask if he could use the telephone.

If this were not all a lie, a re-creation or manipulation of the facts, and if I were the boy who had chased the other boy through the cane, rather than the boy who had leapt into the muddy bayou, then what I would have done, what I should have done, was something heroic: I would have held out my hands like an Indian chief, stopping the other boys from jumping in and swimming after him, or even from gloating. I would have said something noble, like, "He got away. Let him go."

I might even have gone home and called Swamp Boy's parents, so that he wouldn't have to lurk in the shadows in some rich person's yard—afraid to walk home through the woods because of the masked gang, but also afraid to go ask to use the phone.

That's what I would have done if I were the boy who chased him, rather than the boy who got chased, and who made that swim. Who kept, and worshiped, those baroque creatures in his aquarium.

I was that boy, and I was the other one too. I was at the edge of fear, the edge of hesitancy, and had not yet—not then—turned back from it.

There's a heavy rain falling today. The swamps are writhing with life.

BARRED OWL

Seven years ago I got divorced and left Kentucky, heading west. I made the Mississippi River in one day, and it just floored me how big it was. I watched the water until sundown. It didn't seem like a river, but a giant brown muscle instead. Two days later, my car threw a rod and I settled in Greeley, Colorado. Nobody in my family has lived this far off our home hill.

I took a job painting dorm rooms at the college here in town. The pay wasn't the best, but I could go to work hungover and nobody bugged me. I liked the quiet of working alone. I went into a room and made it a different color. The walls and the ceiling hadn't gone anywhere, but it was a new place. Only the view from the window stayed the same. What I did was never look out.

Every day after work I stopped by the Pig's Eye, a bar with cheap draft, a pool table, and a jukebox. It was the kind of place to get drunk in safely, because the law watched student bars downtown. The biggest jerk in the joint was the bartender. He liked to throw people out. You could smoke reefer in the Pig, gamble and fight, but if you drank too much, you were barred. That always struck me odd—like throwing someone out of a hospital for being sick.

Since my social life was tied to the Pig, I was surprised when a man came to the house one Saturday afternoon. That it was Tarvis surprised me even more. He's from eastern Kentucky, and people often mentioned him, but we'd never met. His hair was short and his beard was long. I invited him in.

"Thank ye, no," he said.

I understood that he knew I was just being polite, that he wouldn't enter my house until my welcome was genuine. I stepped outside, deliberately leaving the door open. What happened next was a ritual the likes of which I'd practically forgotten, but once it began, felt like going home with an old girlfriend you happened to meet in a bar.

We looked each other in the eyes for a spell.

Tarvis nodded slightly.

I nodded slightly.

He opened a pouch of Red Man and offered a chew.

I declined and began the slow process of lighting a cigarette while he dug a wad of tobacco from the pouch.

I flicked the match away, and we watched it land.

He worked his chew and spat, and we watched it hit in

the grass. Our hands were free. We'd shown that our guard was down enough to watch something besides each other.

"Nice house," he said.

"I rent."

"Weather ain't too awful bad this spring."

"Always use rain."

"Keep dogs?" he said.

"Used to."

"Fish?"

"Every chance I get."

He glanced at me and quickly away. It was my turn now. If you don't hear an accent you lose it, and just being around him made me talk like home.

"Working hard?" I said.

"Loafing."

"Get home much?"

"Weddings and funerals."

"I got it down to funerals myself," I said.

"Only place I feel at home anymore is the graveyard."

He spat again, and I stubbed out my cigarette. A half moon had been hanging in the sky since late afternoon as if waiting for its chance to move.

"Hunt?" he asked.

I spat then, a tiny white dab near his darker pool, mine like a star, his an eclipse. I hadn't hunted since moving here. Hunters in the West used four-wheel-drive go-carts with a gunrack on the front and a cargo bin behind. They lived in canvas wall-tents that had woodstoves and cots. I'd seen them coming and going like small armies in the mountains. People at home hunted alone on foot. Tarvis looked every inch a hunter and I decided not to get into it with him.

"Not like I did," I said.

He nodded and looked at me straight on, which meant the reason for his visit was near.

"Skin them out yourself?" he said.

I nodded.

"Come by my place tomorrow, then."

He gave me directions and drove away, his arm hanging out the window. I figured he needed help dressing out a deer. I'm not big on poaching but with the deer already dead, refusing to help meant wasting the meat.

I headed for the bar, hoping to meet a woman. The problem with dating in a college town is that the young women are too young, and the older ones usually have kids. I've dated single mothers but it's hard to know if you like the woman or the whole package. A ready-made home can look awful good. Women with kids tell me it's just as tricky for them. Men figure they're either hunting a full-time daddy or some overnight action, with nothing in between.

This night was the usual Pig crowd, my friends of seven years. I drank straight shots and at last call ordered a couple of doubles. I'd started out drinking to feel good but by the end I was drinking not to feel anything. During the drive home I had to look away from the road to prevent the center stripe from splitting. I fixed that by straddling it. In the morning I woke fully dressed on my couch.

Four cigarettes and a cup of coffee later I felt alive enough to visit Tarvis. He lived below town on a dirt road beside the South Platte River. I veered around a dead raccoon with a tire trench cut through its guts. There were a couple of trailers and a few small houses. Some had outdoor toilets. At Tarvis's house I realized why the area seemed both strangely foreign and familiar. It was a little version of eastern Kentucky, complete with woodpiles, cardboard windows, and a lousy road. The only thing missing was hills.

I'd woke up still drunk and now that I was getting sober, the hangover was coming on. I wished I'd brought some beer. I got nervous that Tarvis had killed his deer in a hard place and needed help dragging it out of the brush. I didn't think I could take it. What I needed was to lie down for a while.

Tarvis came around the house from the rear.

"Hidy," he said. "Ain't too awful late, are ye?"

"Is it on the property?"

He led me behind the house to a line of cottonwoods overlooking the river's floodplain. A large bag lay on a work table. Tarvis reached inside and very gently, as if handling eggs, withdrew a bird. The feathers on its chest made a pattern of brown and white—a barred owl. Its wings spanned four feet. The head feathers formed a widow's peak between the giant eyes. It had a curved yellow beak and inch-long talons. Tarvis caressed its chest.

"Beaut, ain't it?" he said. "Not a mark on her."

"You kill it?"

"No. Found it on the interstate up by Fort Morgan. It hit a truck or something. Neck's broke."

The sun had risen above the trees, streaming heat and light against my face. Owls were protected by the government. Owning a single feather was illegal, let alone the whole bird.

"I want this pelt," Tarvis said.

"Never done a bird."

"You've skinned animals out. Can't be that big a difference."

"Why don't you do it yourself then?"

Tarvis backstepped as an expression close to guilt passed across his face.

"I never skinned nothing," he said. "Nobody taught me on account of I never pulled the trigger. I was raised to it, but I just wasn't able."

I looked away to protect his dignity. His words charged me with a responsibility I couldn't deny, the responsibility of Tarvis's shame. Leaving would betray a confidence that had taken a fair share of guts to tell.

I felt dizzy, but I rolled my sleeves up and began with the right leg. Surrounding the claws were feathers so dense and fine that they reminded me of fur. To prevent tearing the papery skin, I massaged it off the meat. Tarvis stood beside me. I held the owl's body and slowly turned it, working the skin free. My arms cooled from the breeze, and I could smell the liquor in my sweat. The hangover was beginning to lift. I snipped the cartilage and tendon surrounding the large wing bone, and carefully exposed the pink muscle. Feathers scraped the plywood like a broom. The owl was giving itself to me, giving its feathered pelt and its greatest gift, that which separated it from us—the wings. In return I'd give it a proper burial.

There is an intensity to skinning, a sense of immediacy. Once you start, you must continue. Many people work fast to get it over with, but I like to take it slow. I hadn't felt this way in a long time and hadn't known I'd missed it.

I eased the skin over the back of the skull. Its right side was caved in pretty bad. The pelt was inside out, connected to the body at the beak, as if the owl was kissing the shadow of its mate. I passed it to Tarvis. He held the slippery skull in one hand and gently tugged the skin free of the carcass.

"Get a shovel," I said.

Tarvis circled the house for a spade and dug a hole beneath a cottonwood. I examined the bird. Both legs, the skull, each wing, its neck and ribs—all were broken. Its head hung from several shattered vertebrae. I'd never seen a creature so clean on the outside and so tore up on the inside. It had died pretty hard.

I built a twig platform and placed the remains in the grave. Tarvis began to spade the dirt in. He tamped it down, mumbling to himself. I reversed the pelt so the feathers were facing out. The body cavity flattened to an empty skin, a pouch with wings that would never fly.

Hand-shaking is not customary among men in eastern Kentucky. We stood apart from one another and nodded, arms dangling, boots scuffing the dirt, as if our limbs were useless without work.

"Got any whiskey?" I said.

"Way I drank gave it a bad name. Quit when I left Kentucky."

"That's when I took it up. What makes you want that owl so bad?"

"It's pure built to hunt. Got three ear holes and it flies silent. It can open and close each pupil separate from the other one. They ain't a better hunter."

"Well," I said. "Reckon you know your owls."

I drove to the bar for a few shots and thought about eating, but didn't want to ruin a ten-dollar drunk with a five-dollar meal. I didn't meet a woman and didn't care. When the bar closed, a bunch of us bought six-packs and went to my house. I laid drunk through most of the week, thinking about Tarvis in the blurred space between hangover and the day's first drink. Though I'd shown him how to skin, I had the feeling he was guiding me into something I'd tried to leave behind.

A few weeks later I met a teacher who was considering a move to Kentucky because it was a place that could use her help. We spent a few nights together. I felt like a test for her, a way of gauging Kentucky's need. I guess I flunked because she moved to South Dakota for a job on a Sioux Reservation.

On Memorial Day I took a six-pack of dog hair to Tarvis's house, parked behind his truck, and opened a beer. At first I wanted to gag, but there's no better buzz than a drink on an empty stomach. I drank half and held it down. The heat spread through my body, activating last night's bourbon. I finished the beer and opened another.

Tarvis came out of the house, blinking against the sun. We went to the riverbank and sat in metal chairs. A great blue heron flew north, its neck curled like a snake ready to strike. The air was quiet. We could have been by the Blue Lick River back home. It felt right to sit with someone of the hills, even if we didn't have a lot to say.

I asked to see the owl and Tarvis reluctantly led me to the door. His eyes were shiny as new dimes. "Ain't nobody been inside in eight years."

The cabin was one room with a sink, range, toilet, and mattress. A woodstove stained from tobacco spit stood in the middle. The only furniture was a tattered couch. Shelves lined every wall, filled with things he'd found in the woods.

A dozen owl pellets lay beside a jumble of antlers. A

variety of bird wings were pinned to the wall. One shelf held sun-bleached bones and another contained thirty or forty jaw bones. Skulls were jammed in—raccoon, fox, deer, a dozen groundhog. Hundreds of feathers poked into wall cracks and knotholes. There were so many feathers that I had the sense of being within the owl pelt turned inside out.

Tarvis pulled a board from the highest shelf. The owl lay on its back, wings stretched full to either side. The claws hung from strips of downy hide. Tarvis had smoothed the feathers into their proper pattern.

"You did a good job," I said.

"Had some help."

"Ever find Indian stuff?"

"All this came from hunting arrowheads," he said. "But I never found one. Maybe I don't know how to look."

"Maybe this is what finds you."

He handed me a stick from one of the shelves. It was eighteen inches long, sanded smooth and feathered at one end. He reached under the couch for a handmade bow.

"That's osage orangewood," he said. "Same as the Indians used. I made them both. Soon's I find me a point I'll be setting pretty."

"You going to hunt with it?"

"No." He looked away. "I don't even kill mosquitoes. What I do is let the spiders go crazy in here. They keep the bugs down and snakes stop the mice. Hawks eat the snakes.

43

Fox kills the duck. An owl hunts everything, but nothing hunts the owl. It's like man."

He put the owl on a shelf and opened the door. We went outside. The staccato of a woodpecker came across the river, each peck distinct as a bell.

"How come you don't hunt?" I said.

He looked at me, then away, and back to me. His eyes were smoky.

"I don't know," he said. "Hear that woodpecker? Take and cut its beak off and it'll pound its face against a tree until it dies. Not hunting does me the same way. But I still can't do it."

The river shimmered in the wind, sunlight catching each tiny cresting wave. A breeze carried the scent of clover and mud. I slipped away to my car.

Work hit a low spell. I was in a dorm I'd painted twice before and could do it blindfolded. The rooms repeated themselves, each one a mirror image of the last. I went in and out of the same room over and over. Sometimes I didn't know where I was, and leaving didn't help because the hall-way was filled with identical doors.

The next time I visited Tarvis, I drank the neck and shoulders out of a fifth while he talked. He was from a fam-ily of twelve. His last name was Eldridge. He grew up on Eldridge Ridge, overlooking Eldridge Creek in Eldridge County. His people numbered so many that they got iden-tified by hair color and their mother's maiden name.

Nobody called him Tarvis. He was Ida Cumbow's fourth boy, a black-headed Eldridge. That's what finally made him leave. No one knew who he was.

Tarvis and I sat till the air was greyed by dusk. Night covered us over. We were like a pair of seashells a long way from the beach. If you held one of us to your ear, you'd hear Kentucky in the distance, but listening to both would put you flat in the woods.

An owl called from the river.

"There's your owl," I said.

"No, that's a great horned. A barred owl getting this far west ain't right."

"Maybe that's why it died."

Tarvis looked at me for a spell, his eyes gleaming in the darkness. He never spoke and I left for the Pig. The ease of Tarvis's company just drove in the fact that I didn't belong out here. Maybe that's why I drank so much that night. I woke up the next day filled with dread, craving water, and with no memory of what had happened at the bar. I used to think not remembering meant I'd had a great time. Now I know it for a bad sign, but a drink can cut that fear like a scythe.

I went back to see Tarvis at the height of summer. The river moved so slowly it seemed to be still, a flat pane of re-flected light. Mosquitoes began to circle my head. Tarvis opened his door, squinting against the sun. He'd lost weight. His hands were crusted with dirt and he reminded me of the old men at home, weary from slant-farming hill-sides that never yielded enough.

We nodded to each other, began the ritual of tobacco. His voice sounded rusty and cracked. He moved his lips before each word, forming the word itself.

"Found one," he said.

I knew immediately what he meant.

"Where?"

"Creek. Four mile downriver. Half mile in."

"Flint?"

His head moved in a slow shake.

"Chert," he said. "No flint in America."

"You make the arrow?"

He shivered. Mosquitoes rose from his body and we looked at each other a long time. He never blinked. I smacked a mosquito against my neck. He compressed his lips and went back inside, softly closing the door.

I spent the rest of the summer drinking and didn't think about Tarvis anymore. For a while I dated a woman, if you can call it that. We drank till the bar closed, then went to her house and tried not to pass out in the middle of everything. It eventually went to hell between us. Everybody said it would. She liked to laugh, though, and nothing else really mattered.

The day we split up, I got drunk at the Pig. Someone was in the men's room, and I went in the women's. It was commonly done. The uncommon part was falling through the window. The bartender didn't ask what happened or if I was hurt, just barred me on the spot. He thought I threw a garbage can through the window. He said that nothing human had broken it, and I wondered what he thought I was.

I took my drinking down the street, but it wasn't the same. I was homesick for the Pig.

A few months later a policeman arrived at my house and I got scared that I'd hit someone with my car. I was always finding fresh dents and scraped paint in the morning. The cop was neckless and blond, officially polite. He asked if I knew Tarvis Eldridge and I nodded. He asked if the deceased had displayed any behavior out of the ordinary and I told him no, wanting to side with Tarvis even dead.

"A will left his house to you," the cop said.

"Maybe he wasn't right when he wrote it."

"We don't think he was," the cop said. "But the house is yours."

He stood to leave, and I asked how Tarvis had died. In a slow, embarrassed fashion, he told me part of it. I went to the county coroner who filled in the gaps. It was his most unusual case, and he talked about it like a man who'd pulled in a ten-inch trout on a dime-store rod.

Tarvis had fastened one end of the bow to an iron plate and screwed the plate to the floor. Guy wires held the bow upright. He fitted an arrow with a chert point into the bow, drew it tight, and braced it. A strip of rawhide ran across the floor to the couch where they found him. All he had to do was pull the leather cord to release the arrow.

His body had been sent home for burial. As much as he'd tried to get out, the hills had claimed him.

I drove to Tarvis's house and gathered his personal stuff—a toothbrush and comb, his tobacco pouch, knife, and hat. I dug a hole beside the owl's grave and dropped it all in. It seemed fitting that he'd have two graves, one here and another in Kentucky. I filled the hole and smoothed the earth and didn't know what to say. Everything I came up with sounded stupid. It was such a small place in the ground. I wasn't burying him, I was covering over how I felt.

I left for town. My neighborhood was neat and clean, like dorm walls after a fresh coat. From the outside, my house looked like all the rest. The refrigerator held lunch-meat, eggs, and milk. The toilet ran unless you jiggled the handle. I didn't even go in. I bought a pint for later and drove to the Pig, forgetting that I'd been barred. I sat in the car outside. The windows of the tavern were brightly lit and I knew everyone in there. I'd not been to the Pig for three months and none of my friends had called me, not a one.

I drove back to Tarvis's road, pulled over, and cut the engine. I hadn't known how tore up the inside of the owl was, and I couldn't tell about Tarvis either. Both of them should have stayed in the woods. It made me wonder if I should have. I opened the whiskey. The smell was quick and strong, and I threw the full bottle out the car window. I don't know why. As soon as I did, I regretted it. The bottle didn't break and I heard the bourbon emptying into the ditch. I knew it wouldn't all run out.

I went down the road and parked in the shadow of Tarvis's house. The river was dark and flat. Long-eared owls were calling to each other, answering and calling. There was one female calling and three males hollering back, which reminded me of the Pig. Maybe Tarvis would still be living if he'd let himself take a drink to get through the hard parts. He'd gotten himself home, though, while I was still stuck out here in the world. I suddenly thought of something that drained me like a shell. I sat in the dark listening to the owls but there was no way for me to get around it. I missed Kentucky more than the Pig.

AMEN

He was born with only one eye and maybe that's why he saw things different than most people. The good eye was dark. The sightless eye was all white and lightly veined.

"There's a god in the light of that eye," Sullie's mother said.

Sullie only saw the man's eye once in her life. It was the night of the big fish and she thought it was more like a pearl or moon than like an eye. And it was all the more unusual because Jack was, after all, only an ordinary man. He had an old man's odor and wasn't always clean.

He carved wood and fished like all the men. With his small hands he carved tree limbs into gentle cats, sleeping dogs, and chickens. And he carved chains to hold them all together.

"It's the only way I can keep a cat and dog in the same room," he joked.

Sullie kept most of his carvings. She watched the shavings pile up on the creaking porch until a breeze blew them into the tall grass or weeds. On a hot windless day they'd fall onto the gold back of the sleeping dog or on its twitching ear. She sat at old Jack's feet and watched and smelled the turpentine odor of wood. His unpatched eye was sharp and black. She could see herself in it, her long skinny legs folded under, her faded dress, dark scraggly hair, all in his one good eye. The other eye was covered, as usual, with a leather patch.

Even then he had been pretty old. His skin was loosening from the bones. He was watching with his clear and black eye how the sky grew to be made of shadows. And some days he didn't have room for one more word so they sat in silence.

The night of the big fish, people had been talking about Jack. He wasn't at the picnic and that was a good invitation to gossip.

"Jesse James was part Chickasaw," said Enoch. "Pete has one of his pistols. Word has it that Pete and Jack are related to the James brothers."

Gladys waved her hand impatiently. She leaned her chair back a little and stuck her chest out. "Go on. That old man?"

"That old man was a pallbearer at Jesse James's funeral, yessir."

"They wouldn't have had an Indian at the funeral, would they?" she asked.

"Look it up. Besides, in his younger days he wore a coal black shirt, even when it was hot. And he had one of them there Arabian horses no one else knew how to ride. And a concho belt made out of real silver. Had a silver saddle horn, too."

Will smiled at the other men. He removed his hat and rubbed back his thick black and gray hair. "That's right. Rumor has it his own brother stole that saddle and belt."

People still kept watch for it, for the stirrups dangling like half-moons and the hammered conchos down the sides. There had also been the horsehair bridle he brought back from Mexico. It was red, black, and white horsehair with two heavy threads of purple running through it. The purple dye had come from seashells. Greek shellfish, someone said, and Jack liked to touch the threads and feel the ocean in them, the white Greek stucco buildings, the blue sky. He liked the purple thread more than all the silver. Almost.

"You wouldn't have crossed him in those days. He won that horse in a contest. The trader said if anyone could ride it, they could have it. Jack got on and rode it. He sure did. And then the trader said he couldn't give it to Jack. 'I'd be broke,' he said. So Jack said, 'Give me fifty dollars.' The man said he didn't have that kind of money. Jack pulled out his pistol and said, 'If I kill you, you won't have no worries about money or horses.' "

Everyone nodded. A couple of old folks said, "Amen,"

like good Baptists do. A cheater was a bad man. Jack's brother killed a man for cheating him out of thirty-eight cents. It didn't sound like much but there wasn't much food in those days and the thief had been an outsider. The old folks then also said, "Amen." They had to feed their own. Not much grew out of the dry Oklahoma soil except pebbles. Word had it that this was just a thin layer of earth over big stone underground mountains. Close to the hot sun and the corn-eating grasshoppers.

And even Sullie had lived through two droughts, a dozen or more black and turquoise tornadoes roiling through the sky, and the year that ended in October. That year cotton grew up out of the soft red soil and it grew tall. At first the old people praised the cotton and said "Amen" to the ground. But it kept growing until it was tall as the houses, even the houses with little attics. It stretched up to the wooden rooftops, above the silvered dry wood.

Jack went out in the mornings looking for signs of blossoms. Every morning he stood at the far end of the field and sang a song to the cotton. Sullie went out behind him and hid in the tall green plants. She heard parts of the song and silence and the cotton whisper and grow. No pale flowers ever bloomed. No hint of anything that would dry and burst open with white soft cotton inside. Jack went out daily. He stood and sang. He walked through the plants as if his steps would force the stems to let out frail blossoms.

Sullie's mother watched from the door. She dried her

hands on the back of her skirt. "I don't think nothing's going to work," She whispered to Sullie and it was true because when October came the taller-than-houses plants froze, turned transparent and then dried a dull yellow. And the banks closed. And the new red mules died of bloat. And Sullie learned to keep silent at the long empty table.

"He even shot his own brother-in-law for beating up his sister. At a picnic just like this one."

"Amen," the women said, good Baptists. They nodded their round dark faces in agreement.

"After that he'd never sit by a window or go in a dark room. Why, he wouldn't even go into a barn unless it had two doors because he was sure the law or someone from the family would get him."

"He was mean, all right, a man to be feared. You'd forget he had such tiny little hands. And he only wore a size two shoe. Don't know how he ran so fast or handled them guns. And all the time turning his head like a rooster to make up for the missing eye."

It grew dark and several men went down to the lake to jack fish. They shined big lights into the water and it attracted fish the same way it paralyzed deer or other land animals. They wouldn't have done it if Jack had been there.

Sullie went down to the water. She was almost a teenager and she liked to watch the big men. She liked their tight jeans and shirts and hats. The women didn't like girls following the men but they forgot about her soon, they were so busy talking about new cotton dresses, their own little children sleeping now on blankets on the hillside. And later they'd talk about women things, men, herbs, seeing Eliza George, the old doctor woman who healed their headaches and helped them get pregnant. Sullie would be back in time to hear about Miss George and how to get pregnant.

But for now she watched the lights shine on the water. And light underneath showing up like sunset. A few miles away in the dark she saw the passing headlights of trucks. She sat in a clump of bushes and trees for a while, then went down to the dark edge of the lake. The men couldn't see into the darkness because of the bright lights in their eyes.

She waded in the warm water. The hem of her dress stuck to her legs. She went a little deeper. She stubbed her toe and felt something move and give way. Whatever it was made a large current and she felt frightened. It was cool and slippery and swam like a large fish. Then it stopped. She reached her hand into the water, wetting even her hair, but it was gone. She felt nothing except the fast motion of water.

She smelled the water. She swam a little and looked at the lights the women kept on the table, and the black trees.

She heard voices of the men out in the center of the lake. "Over there," someone said. And the lights swayed on the water.

Jack walked down to the lake. Sullie started to call to him

but then kept still. In the moonlight she saw that he wasn't wearing his eyepatch. And he walked still like maybe he was mad. So she kept silent and waded a littler farther into rocks and weeds and darkness near the shore.

He didn't have a boat or canoe and he stood a moment at the edge of the dark water. Then he dunked himself and stood again. Sullie saw his knobby shoulders beneath the wet shirt, the bones at the neck. Then he submerged himself in the water and swam toward the other men. There were only a few splashes, an occasional glimpse of his head rising out of the water.

Before he reached the men with lights, Sullie heard them all become noisy at once. "Lordy," one of them said. The water near them grew furious and violent. One small canoe tipped and the lights shone off in all directions.

Sullie waded out again to her chest to watch, forgetting about the women's talk. She heard the men's voices. "I could put my hands in that gill slit." Someone else said, "Watch his fins. They're like razor blades." They were pulling something around, taking ropes out of the boats when Jack arrived. Sullie didn't hear the conversation between Jack and the other men but she saw him breathing hard in one of the boats and then he was gone, swimming again toward shore, her direction.

"Pry it out of those rocks," Enoch yelled.

The men were jubilant, dredging up the old fish with only one eye. It was an old presence in the lake and Jack must have known about it all along. His absence had given the younger men permission to fish with illegal light.

He came up from the water close to Sullie and walked through the rocks and sand out into the night air.

Sullie followed Jack a ways. In the darkness there was a tree standing in moonlight, the moon like a silver concho. Jack's hands were small and the light outlined the bones and knuckles. They were spotted like the sides of the ancient fish.

She held herself back from the old man. His shoulders were high and she remembered how he had made cornbread on the day of her birth and fed her honey so she'd never be thin. Sullie's mother had been surprised that Sullie knew this. "Who told you?" she asked.

"Nobody."

"You remember it on your own? Babies can't see."

"I just remember, that's all."

And now he stood breathing in the dark. And there were yucca plants at his feet. After the first freeze they would scatter a circle of black seeds on the earth like magic. Like the flying wisteria seeds that had hit and scared Sullie one night. So much mystery in the world, in the way seeds take to air and mimosa leaves fold in delicate prayer at night.

"Who's there?" he said.

"It's me." Her voice was weak. She was afraid to go near him, afraid to run off. He turned and the sight of his eye made her pull her breath too fast into her lungs. It was bright as the moon and the lanterns on water. He watched her a moment and then turned. He looked toward where the cotton was growing this year, toward a few scattered houses with dark windows. Fireflies appeared while he stood. And the sounds of locusts and crickets Sullie hadn't noticed before.

"Let's go back to the rest of the folks," he said.

And they walked, the skinny wet girl, the skinny wet man. The women shut up when they saw them coming. The men didn't notice. They were dragging the rope-bound old fish up on the shore and all the children were awake and running and splashing the water.

Its fins slowed. The gills quit opening while they cut at it and cleaned it of red and yellow ropey intestines and innards. Dogs lapped at its juices.

In the moonlight the sharp scales were scraped off like hunks of mica in a shining glassy pile.

The smell of fish cooking. The dogs eating parts of the head. So large, that dull-colored thing. They'd all talk about it forever. Something that had survived the drought, the famine, the tornadoes and dead crops. It grew large. It was older than all of them. It had hooks in it and lived.

Sullie refused to eat. She pushed her dish away. Her mother hit the table with a pot. "Eat," she said.

Jack's one eye looked far inside Sullie. She was growing old. She could feel it. In his gaze, she grew old. She grew silent inside. She pulled the plate toward her and looked at the piece of fish, the fried skin and pale bones of it.

"Eat it." Jack motioned with his fork, his own cheeks full of the pink meat. "Eat it. It's an Indian fish."

"Amen," said the women just like they'd always been good Baptists.

MARGARET ATWOOD

My Life As a Bat

1. REINCARNATION

In my previous life I was a bat.

If you find previous lives amusing or unlikely, you are not a serious person. Consider: a great many people believe in them, and if sanity is a general consensus about the content of reality, who are you to disagree?

Consider also: previous lives have entered the world of commerce. Money can be made from them. *You were Cleopatra, you were a Flemish duke, you were a Druid priestess*, and money changes hands. If the stock market exists, so must previous lives.

In the previous-life market, there is not such a great demand for Peruvian ditch-diggers as there is for Cleopatra; or for Indian latrine-cleaners, or for 1952 housewives living in California split-levels. Similarly, not many of us choose to remember our lives as vultures, spiders, or rodents, but some of us do. The fortunate few. Conventional wisdom has it that reincarnation as an animal is a punishment for past sins, but perhaps it is a reward instead. At least a resting place. An interlude of grace.

Bats have a few things to put up with, but they do not inflict. When they kill, they kill without mercy, but without hate. They are immune from the curse of pity. They never gloat.

2. NIGHTMARES

I have recurring nightmares.

In one of them, I am clinging to the ceiling of a summer cottage while a red-faced man in white shorts and a white V-necked T-shirt jumps up and down, hitting at me with a tennis racket. There are cedar rafters up here, and sticky flypapers attached with tacks, dangling like toxic seaweeds. I look down at the man's face, foreshortened and sweating, the eyes bulging and blue, the mouth emitting furious noise, rising up like a marine float, sinking again, rising as if on a swell of air.

The air itself is muggy, the sun is sinking; there will be a thunderstorm. A woman is shrieking, "My hair! My hair!" and someone else is calling, "Anthea! Bring the stepladder!" All I want is to get out through the hole in the screen, but that will take some concentration and it's hard in this din of voices, they interfere with my sonar. There is a smell of dirty bathmats—it's his breath, the breath that comes out from every pore, the breath of the monster. I will be lucky to get out of this alive.

In another nightmare I am winging my way—flittering, I suppose you'd call it—through the clean-washed demilight before dawn. This is a desert. The yuccas are in bloom, and I have been gorging myself on their juices and pollen. I'm heading to my home, to my home cave, where it will be cool during the burnout of day and there will be the sound of water trickling through limestone, coating the rock with a glistening hush, with the moistness of new mushrooms, and the other bats will chirp and rustle and doze until night unfurls again and makes the hot sky tender for us.

But when I reach the entrance to the cave, it is sealed over. It's blocked in. Who can have done this?

I vibrate my wings, sniffing blind as a dazzled moth over the hard surface. In a short time the sun will rise like a balloon on fire and I will be blasted with its glare, shriveled to a few small bones.

Whoever said that light was life and darkness nothing? For some of us, the mythologies are different.

3. VAMPIRE FILMS

I became aware of the nature of my previous life gradually, not only through dreams but through scraps of memory, through hints, through odd moments of recognition.

There was my preference for the subtleties of dawn and dusk, as opposed to the vulgar blaring hour of high noon. There was my déjà vu experience in the Carlsbad Caverns—surely I had been there before, long before, before they put in the pastel spotlights and the cute names for stalactites and the underground restaurant where you can combine claustrophobia and indigestion and then take the elevator to get back out.

There was also my dislike for headfuls of human hair, so like nets or the tendrils of poisonous jellyfish: I feared entanglements. No real bat would ever suck the blood of necks. The neck is too near the hair. Even the vampire bat will target a hairless extremity—by choice a toe, resembling as it does the teat of a cow.

Vampire films have always seemed ludicrous to me, for this reason but also for the idiocy of their bats—huge rubbery bats, with red Christmas-light eyes and fangs like a saber-toothed tiger's, flown in on strings, their puppet wings flapped sluggishly like those of an overweight and degenerate bird. I screamed at these filmic moments, but not with fear; rather with outraged laughter, at the insult to bats.

O Dracula, unlikely hero! O flying leukemia, in your cloak like a living umbrella, a membrane of black leather which you unwind from within yourself and lift like a stripteaser's fan as you bend with emaciated lust over the neck, flawless and bland, of whatever woman is longing for obliteration, here and now in her best negligee. Why was it given to you by whoever stole your soul to transform yourself into bat and wolf, and only those? Why not a vampire chipmunk, a duck, a gerbil? Why not a vampire turtle? Now that would be a plot.

4. THE BAT AS A DEADLY WEAPON

During the Second World War they did experiments with bats. Thousands of bats were to be released over German cities, at the hour of noon. Each was to have a small incendiary device strapped onto it, with a timer. The bats would have headed for darkness, as is their habit. They would have crawled into holes in walls, or secreted themselves under the eaves of houses, relieved to have found safety. At a pre-ordained moment they would have exploded, and the cities would have gone up in flames.

That was the plan. Death by flaming bat. The bats too would have died, of course. Acceptable megadeaths.

The cities went up in flames anyway, but not with the aid of bats. The atom bomb had been invented, and the fiery bat was no longer thought necessary.

If the bats had been used after all, would there have been a war memorial to them? It isn't likely.

If you ask a human being what makes his flesh creep more, a bat or a bomb, he will say the bat. It is difficult to experience loathing for something merely metal, however ominous. We save these sensations for those with skin and flesh: a skin, a flesh, unlike our own.

5. BEAUTY

Perhaps it isn't my life as a bat that was the interlude. Perhaps it is this life. Perhaps I have been sent into human form as if on a dangerous mission, to save and redeem my own folk. When I have gained a small success, or died in the attempt—for failure, in such a task and against such odds, is more likely—I will be born again, back into that other form, that other world where I truly belong.

More and more, I think of this event with longing. The quickness of heartbeat, the vivid plunge into the nectars of crepuscular flowers, hovering in the infrared of night; the dank lazy half-sleep of daytime, with bodies rounded and soft as furred plums clustering around me, the mothers licking the tiny amazed faces of the newborn; the swift love of what will come next, the anticipation of the tongue and of the infurled, corrugated and scrolled nose, nose like a dead leaf, nose like a radiator grille, nose of a denizen of Pluto.

And in the evening, the supersonic hymn of praise to our Creator, the Creator of bats, who appears to us in the form of a bat and who gave us all things: water and the liquid stone of caves, the woody refuge of attics, petals and fruit and juicy insects, and the beauty of slippery wings and sharp white canines and shining eyes.

What do we pray for? We pray for food as all do, and for health and for the increase of our kind; and for deliverance from evil, which cannot be explained by us, which is hair-headed and walks in the night with a single white unseeing eye, and stinks of half-digested meat, and has two legs.

Goddess of caves and grottoes: bless your children.

PAULINE MELVILLE

ERZULIE

"I want to get out of here," mumbled Mrs. Rita Jenkins, previously Miss Rita Rimpersaud, as she lumbered like a tank from the bathroom into the living-room. Her husband stood reading his newspaper against the light from the window. There were tears in her eyes as she repeated the information with a hiccuping sob.

"I want to leave."

She has just lowered herself on to the toilet only to have her broad behind greeted by a flight of frogs from the toilet bowl.

Armand Jenkins lowered the paper and looked at her with the expression of helpless exasperation that he kept in store for such occasions. He blinked at her several times to indicate blameless bewilderment. His wife was the only person who could induce in him this mien of defencelessness, of not knowing quite what to do. He rather enjoyed it. It made him feel like a little boy again.

At work, there was no room for any such hints of vulnerability or indecision.

"But, honey, you said you wanted to come—that you were longing to see the old place again," he almost pleaded.

Rita Jenkins sat on the taut surface of a sofa expensively covered in pink-and-mauve chintz. It just managed to resist her weight, indenting slightly. There were three of these giant sofas in the living-room with arms and cushions shaped like stone boulders. The imposing sofas formed three sides of a square which contained a glass coffee table.

"I did," she whined, "but frogs just jumped out of the toilet. I forgot about frogs." She wrinkled her brown nose in distaste. Her shoulders lifted and dropped again. "And I miss Sally." Their daughter had remained behind in Canada to study garden landscaping. She pursed her lips and tried to look pathetic—difficult in one whose solid expanse of chest formed such an unassailable frontispiece.

When Rita's husband had been posted to Guyana to supervise the operations of Omai Gold Mining Ltd., an offshoot of Canadian parent companies, Cambior and Golden Star Resources, she had been delighted at the thought of meeting old school chums again and catching up on their news. At the age of twenty-one she had migrated from Guyana to Canada with her family who were wealthy Guyanese jewellers. Two years later, she married an equally wealthy Canadian mining engineer, Armand Jenkins. Twenty years after that, when her husband's work required him to spend some time in Guyana, she jumped at the chance to return and show off a little in front of her less fortunate contemporaries.

On their return, the Jenkinses rented part of an enormous, gracious, old-style house in Main Street. The Canadian company paid for their living area to be refurbished throughout. As the house boasted some twenty rooms, far too many for the two of them, they only used the second floor. The rest of the house remained a dusty monument to the days of its past glory, full of ancient dressers, old local paintings, curios and knick-knacks, including an Amerindian skull the top of which had been carved as a lid for use as a vanity box. There was even a four-poster bed in one room. Rita could be heard schlep-schlepping heavily along the corridors in her half-slippers, checking for dust or disorder in her own quarters. The rest of the house she ignored.

"Either my nose is paranoid or this bathroom smells unhealthy," she complained to the housekeeper, Adèle, as she sniffed around the place for bad odours. But, on the whole, Rita luxuriated as of old in the warmth of the climate and the free flow of breezes in the house after her severely air-conditioned abode in Canada. The staff, who arrived daily, outnumbered the occupants by five.

Back in Guyana once more, Rita Jenkins greeted past acquaintances with warmth, curiosity, and the satisfaction which came with seeing how much more prosperous than them she had become. This state of affairs made her bountiful.

"Have it. Keep it. Go on, it's yours," she would say, simpering, smiling and nodding encouragement as one of her friends looked longingly at a silk blouse hanging in the walk-in wardrobe or stroked the head of a small wooden sculpture. From the kitchen, the sound of the mixer whizzing up rum swizzles, in the way that Rita liked them with milk and a little essence of vanilla, signalled the arrival of elevenses. The drinks were usually served on a silver tray in the parlour by Margot, the solid deaf-mute servant employed on a casual basis by Adèle the housekeeper.

Now it was nine months after her arrival and Rita had had enough. Armand's contract was for two years. He spent long periods away at Omai, supervising the mining operations. She was bored. The novelty had worn off. She wanted to return to Canada. Apart from the constant electricity blackouts and water cuts, she had recently begun to receive a series of unsettling phone calls on their private and ex-directory number.

"Hello, I'm calling from Berbice." The unknown woman's voice was high and obsequious.

"Who is this, please?" a puzzled Rita had enquired.

"Oh don' worry wid dat. I just want to talk to you. Is your husband there? You're so nice. How have you been today?"

"I think you must have the wrong number."

"Is that the residence of Mr. and Mrs. Armand Jenkins?"

"Yes. This is our private number. If you wish to talk about official business please call the offices of Omai Gold Mining Ltd. during office hours."

"No. It's all right. I just wanted to have a little talk. How you doing?"

"What is it that you want?" Rita was becoming slightly unnerved. "Is it a visa to Canada?" Armand Jenkins was known to have influence in obtaining those precious Canadian visas.

"Not really. I just wanted to know that everything is going through OK with you. Just a little 'Hi and Bye' call. I'll check next week and see that things are going along fine. Good-bye."

There had been several such calls from the woman Rita Jenkins referred to as "the mad lady from Berbice."

She sulked on the sofa. Armand had gone back to reading his newspaper. Rita shook off her sandals and planted her broad, bare feet on the floor. Bored and under-occupied, she reached for a chocolate from the blue ceramic dish on the coffee table, persuading herself that she must eat them in order to prevent them melting.

"And then there's that awful Shallow-Grave case," grumbled Rita, shuddering as she put her feet up on the sofa and munched.

"I'm just reading about it," said Armand, engrossed in the paper.

⤳

The woman was known as Shallow-Grave because that was the way she disposed of her victims, or alleged victims, along the banks of the Essequibo River.

The first body to be discovered was that of a sailor who disappeared from his Filipino ship while it was docked for repairs. The ship had been bringing, amongst other cargoes, some of the cyanide compounds necessary for the mining company at Omai. No one could guess how the unfortunate victim had made his last journey from Tiger Bay to the banks of the Essequibo near Supenaam. But one month later, the great tidal river nudged him back to the sandy surface of the river shore about half a mile from the village of Good Hope. Others followed.

Even in a country with a river for a backbone, where surprise offerings were frequently thrown up to the villagers who lived on its shores, no one was prepared for the assortment of corpses which the river put on display along its edge over the next few months: three fishermen, two foreign seamen, and a surveyor who had been measuring the volumetric discharge and tidal flow of the waters. Shouts were raised on the stretch of river between the villages of Makeshift and Perseverance, usually by those doing a spot of night-fishing, as each new discovery was made. There had been eight corpses in all. Nobody knew the total count.

In Georgetown, where the case was being heard, people

flocked to the courtroom to see for themselves the tall, stately woman accused of this string of murders. The public gallery groaned and heaved with men and women sweating, jostling, fanning themselves and jockeying for the best position to catch a glimpse of the woman who stood in the dock.

She remained elegant and dignified, somewhat aloof, with a cool demeanour that made many of the onlookers in the gallery appear to be more likely candidates for the charges made against her. People strained forward, not only to get a better look, but as if, by reaching closer, they might be able to dip into one of the blackwater creeks of the Essequibo region and escape the broiling heat. The air surrounding her seemed to be of a considerably lower temperature than the air in the rest of the courtroom. When Shallow-Grave leaned forward, the crowd leaned forward. When Shallow-Grave left the room at lunchtime, the atmosphere returned to one of habble and babble and clatter, everyday business and heat, the black radiance of a dark lake having moved elsewhere.

One woman in the public gallery never took her eyes from Shallow-Grave. It was Margot, the sixty-year-old deaf-mute who had not missed one day of the trial. Round her broad-domed head, which was slightly too large for her body, she tied the same faded triangular grey headscarf in a tight band so that no hair showed. Her large head made her powerful hands and arms seem disproportionately short and stubby. Her complexion was matt black with a porous quality like pumice stone, which never shone and seemed to absorb heat. Her mouth, pink and wet as a water-melon, always remained slightly open. She wore an old grey sweat-stained T-shirt and sat in the front row with her elbows on her knees and her chin resting on her fists, concentrating intently on the figure in the dock.

Before she found work with the Jenkinses, Margot used to walk every day from Werk-en-Rust to Subryanville to wash and iron for a lawyer and his wife, both of whom did good works. They paid her too little and she left. She took in washing and ironing at home but a nagging pain in her right arm forced her to stop. Now she lived on a pittance made from the few hours of domestic work she could find. Three mornings a week, she helped out in the kitchen of the Jenkinses' rented house in Main Street.

The rest of the staff were curious about Margot, not least because she had mysteriously disappeared for a month recently and arrived back without a word of explanation. They also maintained a prurient interest in Margot's reaction to her Great Disappointment. Everyone knew that for years Margot had nursed an overpowering desire to migrate to Brooklyn. She shook and trembled when she thought of Brooklyn. Brooklyn was her Holy Grail. When she walked the streets of Georgetown, whether in stupefying heat or tropical downpour, her mind and hopes were pinned on Brooklyn. She was what is known as "waiting to be sent for." In other words, a friend of hers had already gone ahead to the United States and had written to Margot telling her that papers had been lodged applying for permission for Margot to join her. That was four years ago.

From that time on, Margot had received no news, either from the American Embassy or from her friend. Mr. and Mrs. Jenkins' housekeeper, Adèle, had once accompanied Margot to the embassy in order to act as interpreter. The two women had inched their way along in a slow-moving line under the blazing sun. But it appeared that the papers had gone missing.

When they returned to the house, Margot resumed her duties with the other women in the kitchen, squeezing grapefruits and pouring the green juice into a glass jug. Adèle tentatively indicated that perhaps the papers had never been lodged in the first place. The outrage that this suggestion raised in Margot, the look of shocked betrayal on her face, prevented Adèle from ever mentioning it again. Margot had dropped the grapefruit and pounded her fists on the table in a passion.

"Ook-in. Ook-in." Her thick lips opened wide and the others glimpsed a stub of pink tongue as she struggled to pronounce the word.

"Ook-in. Ook-in," she continued in a shouting grunt. And then, amidst general laughter, the other women noticed that Margot's face was streaming with tears.

No one quite understood what was happening to Margot.

She did not fully understand it herself. But what Adèle had said struck her with terror as she finally realised she was not going anywhere. With all her daydreams of a future in Brooklyn smashed, she had begun to wander around Georgetown and see, as if for the first time, the situation in which life had placed her.

She saw streets of tumbling, ramshackle houses, hutches and sheds, slum dwellings tacked together with criss-cross pieces of fencing, and she felt as though she herself had become as dry and sucked of moisture as the sun-bleached grey timbers. Her own headscarf too was grey with wear and sweat. When she chanced to catch sight of it, her large face looked grey, the colour of old lava. The greyness was all around her and everything inside her too seemed to have crumbled into grey dust. Her shoes had more or less disintegrated, peeling open like old, blackened banana skins in their unequal battle against unpaved roads, stones, rains, mud, sun, and dust. Every alley had its own stench of frying food, of fly-infested garbage, stagnant pools, and rotting planks. She felt like a ghost in her own city. A jumbie. Nobody seemed to notice her. She could have been invisible.

When she was arrested for trying to sell some cans of paint that turned out to have been stolen, she took no evasive action. She just raised her large head and looked up at the policeman with incomprehension, her mouth open, as if she were raking his face for an explanation not just of her

arrest, but of her whole predicament. She had allowed herself to be taken quietly to the lock-up at La Penitence and
sat, patient and defeated, through all the procedures that
brought her finally to the women's jail in New Amsterdam
to serve a month's sentence.

It was in the jail that she met Shallow-Grave.

Shallow-Grave occupied one of the three special cells reserved for notorious or first-degree criminals. On the few
occasions when the other women came anywhere near
her—for she had her own special escort—they noticed that
Shallow-Grave was always clean and smelt good. There
was something sparkling about her. And she sang beautifully, in her cell, with a voice that was sometimes low and
husky but ranged upwards to a clear, rippling, thrilling
soprano.

One day when Margot stood in the courtyard with four
other inmates, Shallow-Grave was unlocked from her cell
and appeared, escorted by a weary-looking, squat prison
officer. She was being taken to empty her chamber-pot in
one of the four stinking latrines at the top of a flight of
wooden stairs to the right of the yard. Margot watched her
as she mounted the rackety steps and pulled open the door
of the cabin. When she emerged, she stood at the top of the
steps, a statuesque figure, with the blue china chamber-pot
glinting in the sun. Against the dried dead wood of the latrines, her skin shone a vibrant black. She wore a shoulder-
less, dark-blue cotton dress, slimline, with a white frill on

the hem like the coastal waves of the Atlantic Ocean. As she surveyed the scene from her vantage point, the women below fell silent. And then she addressed them.

"I swear before the sky above and the earth below that I am innocent. I want you all to carry the news when you return to Georgetown and print it in the *Chronicle* and the *Stabroek News.* I know what everybody does call me. But my name is Erzulie."

The announcement took her escort by surprise and she tried to chivvy her charge along and down the steps. There were strict rules about Shallow-Grave not having contact with the other women. But Shallow-Grave remained composed and she slowly descended the stairs in her own time. When she reached the bottom, she first looked up at the sky and then knelt to kiss the ground before proceeding calmly on her way. She ignored the admonitions of the prison guard at her side. As she passed the other women, the air became fresh with a zingy, salty sort of smell and they could see her lick what looked like grains of salt from her lips.

For Margot, seeing the gleaming statuesque figure on top of the stairs, with the bright blue sky stretching away behind her, was an epiphany. From that moment on, Margot knew that it was through Shallow-Grave that she would find her salvation.

Shallow-Grave's diet proved to be a problem for the authorities. Fish was the main fare in the prison, every sort of fish, fish soup that looked like grey fluff floating in the dish, even fish water to drink. But Shallow-Grave found shrimps and unscaled fish distasteful and pushed anything like that to the side of her plate. Rice-pap and bush tea were acceptable to her. Eventually, because of her commanding presence, some of the warders found themselves sneaking in fruit for her.

All the women in the jail craved fresh fruit and vegetables. Fights broke out in the dormitory over whose turn it was to tend the kitchen garden. Although the produce from the garden was scanty and destined for sale elsewhere, it was sometimes possible to smuggle a piece of callaloo or some peppers which, if not eaten, could be exchanged for tobacco. Every morning the inmates recited the Guyana pledge and sang the national anthem. The ration of water was given out each day. Everyone had a five-pound milk tin to hold the water and it was an art to use it effectively.

To the annoyance of Miss Vinny and the kitchen squad, who were taken to bathe in the stone communal bath after Shallow-Grave had completed her ablutions, it seemed that Shallow-Grave had an inexhaustible supply of water, for the whole bath remained damp and glistening with drips. Miss Vinny would suck her teeth at the sight of it.

Miss Vinny was a sixty-seven-year-old ex-Sunday-school teacher and a murderess in her own right. She was one of the longest-serving prisoners and resented the attention and respect that Shallow-Grave attracted. She scowled and fixed her glasses. Her hair, scraped back and tied with a scrap of cloth, stuck out at the back like the bristles of a yard brush.

"That woman gettin' favours," grumbled Miss Vinny. "All this rabble in here. They all criminals," she confided to some subdued new inmates who had been relieved to find that, although the dormitory windows were barred, the dormitory was reasonably fresh and airy.

With noises and signs, Margot did her best to obtain what information she could about her new idol. At first, she made contact with Shallow-Grave through her enormous shy smile. Later, she proved her devotion by giving Shallow-Grave cigarettes and fruit which she smuggled through the grille of her cell window. Margot thought Shallow-Grave the most devastatingly beautiful and impressive creature she had ever seen. Shallow-Grave received all this attention graciously as if it were her due. Once Margot found the stub of an old candle and passed it through to Shallow-Grave. In this new passion of servitude, Margot felt herself coming alive again. Anything she could find, she delivered to Shallow-Grave, even if it was the bluey-mauve jacaranda petals shed by the tree just outside the wire netting of the prison enclosure.

Shallow-Grave continued to accept this service as if it were rightfully hers. But she sang more often and some miracle cleared Margot's ears of the buffeting winds that normally blew there and enabled her to hear Shallow-Grave's soothing voice:

Them that's got shall get,
Them that don't shall lose.

Margot lay on her bed in a rapture. The matter was sealed as far as she was concerned. From then on she was the devoted servant of Shallow-Grave.

Lock-down time was half past three. Late one afternoon as dusk began to fall over the prison, an East Indian woman known as "Catchme Latchmi" who had been found guilty of smuggling a hundred cans of Nestlé's milk into the country, hung on to the bar listening to Shallow-Grave singing:

If you can't see the one you love,
Love the one you're with.

Miss Vinny was sitting in a sulk on her bed because the newcomers she had befriended were apparently related to a government minister and Matron had insisted that their beds were to be specially made up with fresh blue sheets and pillows in contrast with the other cots. Miss Vinny had only been mollified by finding a Georgetown telephone number in Margot's kitchen-apron pocket, a number which she intended to use at some time in the future.

Suddenly, Latchmi yelled, "Miss. Miss. Come quick."

Through the window, in the dusk, she had spotted a snake undulating swiftly across the courtyard in the direction of the special cells. Soon, one of the warders was hurrying across the yard with a kerosene lamp. When she opened up Shallow-Grave's cell, she was greeted by the sight of Shallow-Grave sitting upright in a pink shortie nightie. It took a few seconds for the warder to realise that Shallow-Grave, still crooning, was caressing the brown-and-yellow paw-paw snake as it twined and wreathed around her neck. The warder, shaking with horror, went to report the matter to her colleagues.

From then on, rumour abounded that Shallow-Grave was, in fact, a water mumma.

When Margot was released, she returned to Georgetown to observe Shallow-Grave's trial. At weekends, unable to bear the separation from her idol, she returned to New Amsterdam. She secured a room in a house in King Street not far from the jail. Margot hoped to be able to catch a glimpse of her idol or smuggle messages to her.

Every Friday, Margot returned to this room. One dark, dingy curtain fluttered at the window. The cupboard on the side was rotting with old woodwork. The bed sheets were patched and greasy with age. The wind brought flecks of grey cane ash through the window. Tiny weightless flies settled on a pair of the owner's damp panties, pegged up in a corner to dry. Outside the door, in the kitchen, stood a flaking stove with rusted canisters of gas under the sink. But she was happy. On her first Friday, through the window, she saw a man behaving oddly. He was standing on tiptoe at the side of a wooden house that was barely standing upright. His arm, up to the shoulder, was reaching through a hole in the side wall. Margot could not figure out what he was doing. Then she realised he was fishing around to see if he could feel anything worth stealing.

Something had gone wrong with New Amsterdam. After its heyday in the last century, the town was now in full rigor mortis. It was a town with memory loss. Street names had dropped off and not been replaced. The buildings were wooden skeletons, leaning against each other as if they had a headache. By the stelling where the ferry plied its trade across the Berbice River, the rusting hulks of sixteen abandoned buses paraded their dereliction, one still displaying its destination in faded letters—Crabwood Creek.

Discussion in the town revolved around health. Half the population had been afflicted with a mysterious condition which resulted in everyone producing white shit with lacy fronds.

"And what is it when you teeth wobble and bleed in you gums?" asked a man buying a slab of cheesy yellow cake from the bakery.

"Me na know," replied the proprietor. "Everybody sick these days. I gat pain an' I vomitin' some stuff yellow like lemon. Somebody done this place something. De whole place gat a spell on it."

The conversation turned to crime.

"You hear what happen in New Street? Dey chloroform dem. Dey woke up on de floor. De bed take away from under dem. Everything gone and dey gat dis sweet, strong taste in dey mouth. When dey run for de police, police say dey caan' come 'cos dey don' got money for gas."

Such stories of a town bewitched ran riot wherever people congregated. One girl came out of her bedroom to find a young woman calmly removing all her clothes from a wardrobe on the landing outside. Another man left a pot of food on the stove for a few minutes and when he returned, the pot of food had been stolen. The town seemed to be in the grip of a nightmare. Worst of all, someone had seen a dog running from the hospital with a package in its mouth. It stopped by a trench to worry the brown parcel open. A nine-inch, semi-transparent human foetus fell out and the dog ran off triumphantly with the embryonic child in its mouth. In the last year, three young couples had crawled under the raised floor of the Catholic church and taken poison.

Margot sat on the bed and tried to work out how to contact Shallow-Grave.

Miss Vinny enjoyed the position of "Trusty Prisoner." She held the privileged and much envied job of cleaning and sweeping out Matron's office once a week. No one knew how she had obtained the private number of Mr. and Mrs.

Armand Jenkins in Georgetown, but every time she went to clean the office, she took the opportunity to use the telephone. She cherished her new-found relationship with Rita Jenkins. Even though it was a rather one-sided friendship, it calmed Miss Vinny. She liked to feel she had a place in the life of the middle classes. It soothed her ego which had to withstand the myriad humiliations of prison life and gave her a satisfying feeling of superiority. The calls, when she could make them, were the highlight of her weekly routine in jail.

"Good morning. I just callin' to find out how you goin' through." Miss Vinny's face contorted with the effort of producing her best standard English. "I hope you not findin' the rain too wet."

She was standing with her back to the doorway, her broom in one hand and the telephone in the other. She did not see Matron enter.

"Put that telephone down immediately."

Miss Vinny dropped her broom with shock. She hung the telephone back on the receiver without saying another word. Matron escorted her along the faded wooden corridor back to the dormitory, scolding and threatening dire punishments. Immediately, on reaching the dormitory, Miss Vinny was stripped of her trusty's arm-band.

Miss Vinny did not take well to this new loss of status. She mumbled constantly to herself. She had been taken off duties in the kitchen garden and was similarly denied access to the administrative offices. She was reduced to being an ordinary prisoner. It did not suit her. She began to brood.

And then, one afternoon in the dormitory after lock-down, a strong wind began to blow through the bars and one of the women got up to close the shutters. Miss Vinny, who had been moping on her bed, got up and grabbed the woman's arm to stop her.

"I goin' catch that wind," she said. "Long time since the wind ain' catch." Her voice had a hard edge of determination. The rest of the women in the dormitory hoisted themselves on their elbows and turned to see what was happening.

Miss Vinny strode over to each window in turn, flinging the shutters open. The jail was not far from the wide Berbice River and the blustering Trade Winds blew through the windows. Soon the room was filled with wind. Some of the women started to remonstrate but Miss Vinny, shaking with what seemed like rage, hurled herself like a tornado from one window to another. For a while she stood at the end window, gulping in enormous amounts of air until she started to breathe fast and heavily in panting wheezes.

And then she reeled over to the centre of the room, her arms extended like a child playing aeroplanes. Her foot stamped down in a regular rhythm and her spine arched. Suddenly, Miss Vinny felt released to do something she realised she had wanted to do for a long time. She no longer yearned to speak to that silly woman in Georgetown. She wanted to do something she remembered her Surinamese grandmother teaching her. The Winti Dance. She wanted to do the Winti Dance. She used the beat of her foot to remember the words her grandmother sang:

Fodu dede, ma a de
Yu kapu en nanga howru
Ma a de.

No sooner had she begun to move around the room than her tongue became empowered with a host of sounds, an extraordinary range of noises. Each new one took her by delighted surprise and affected the movements of her body. Each one flung her into a different position to a subtly changed rhythm. She had tapped into a stream of energy. Sometimes the noise turned her into a tall, powerful man with a limp and sometimes into an undulating, hip-winding woman. At the age of sixty-seven, Miss Vinny opened herself up joyously to the whole pantheon of creation.

As she wheeled around the centre of the dormitory, Savitri, a heavy woman with dark circles under her eyes, who was prone to depression, rose from her bed, moaning and breathing heavily. She and two other women began to writhe on the floor as if they were trying to slough off their skins. They were tended spontaneously by women trying to ensure they did not hurt themselves and then some of these attendants also began to succumb to the spirits.

By the time the warden had summoned help, most of the women in the dormitory were possessed by an intoxicating and exhilarating frenzy. One or two were in a trance. Only the three newcomers huddled together in a corner, crying, unable to join in.

It took five prison wardens to calm the women down. Some fell across their beds in a state of extreme exhaustion, lethargy, or sleep. Gradually, the ecstasies subsided and the prisoners dozed or giggled and looked at one another sheepishly until they too fell asleep to the sound of Shallow-Grave's voice singing from her cell. That night, the special escort was taken away from Shallow-Grave's cell in order that as many guards as possible should be available to protect the dormitory from another such outbreak.

Next morning, the resident psychiatrist from the asylum down the road prepared to leave for his weekly visit to the women's jail. He had fled Singapore after some irregularities in his practice were uncovered. As he left he checked the blackboard in the entrance lobby which had the current figures chalked on it:

In-patients—63
Out-patients—143
Escaped—426

He sighed as he walked towards the jail for his weekly surgery. What could he do with old medicines that had lost their potency? He could not even get hold of the latest scientific papers.

When he reached the jail, he was turned away. Everything was in uproar. Shallow-Grave had escaped.

It had been Margot's brainwave to organise Shallow-Grave's escape. It was she who had concealed her mistress in the toilets below deck as the rusty ferry ploughed its way across the Berbice River to Rossignol. And it was her brilliant idea to secrete Shallow-Grave in one of the many unused rooms of the house in Main Street where the Jenkinses rented their apartment.

At nights, Margot slipped out and padded along the creaking corridors, over the gleaming wooden floors, past the solid circular staircase, to fetch bowls of water, soft towels and soap for her mistress.

In her concealed room, Shallow-Grave reclined on a single bed covered by the deep-rose silken bedspread which Margot had, many times, washed and ironed. Sometimes it seemed to Margot that the purpose of past actions is only revealed later. She had always washed and ironed that coverlet with particular care without knowing why. Now she understood. She brushed and teased her mistress's black, wiry hair which spread like bladder-wrack seaweed in profusion on the pillow. She massaged her gleaming cheeks, neck, and shoulders and Shallow-Grave accepted all these ministrations like an empress.

Beside the bed, the electric fan rolled its head to and fro

like a metal sunflower slowly following the sun. Shallow-
Grave liked to be kept cool. Margot often bathed her as she
lay naked on the bed. She would lift her leg, tenderly washing the private parts that amazed her with their resemblance to a great purple sea-anemone.

Margot slept on the floor between the door and her
charge. During the night she would go and purloin what
food she could for them both. No one noticed the creaking
of her footsteps down the passages at night because the
house produced its own creaks and rustles even when there
was no one there. They breakfasted on slices of paw-paw,
crackers and cheese, whatever she had been able to scav-
enge. Margot barely allowed her eyes to leave Shallow-
Grave's face as they both ate, so hugely did she enjoy
Shallow-Grave's pleasure.

Once she took the risk of staying in the kitchen for an
extra hour, squeezing the green transparent tears from
grapefruit, and brought the juice back on a tray, served in
a huge wine goblet with crushed ice from the freezer.
Before dawn, Margot carried bowls containing her mistress's shit and golden urine and emptied them down one
of the toilets, flushing it with a bucket of water when necessary.

The house provided everything. There was no need to
leave the premises and risk discovery. Margot had become
adept at showing herself during the day as usual when she
was expected for work. At the day's end, she pretended to

leave and just waited for an opportunity to slip back into her hiding place.

Mostly, they stayed in the room during the day with the Demerara shutters open. The room was too high for anyone to see from the path below. When there was a power outage and the electric fan stopped, Margot fanned Shallow-Grave with a fan of dried woven reeds that she had found on the floor above. Cupboards of dark-red crabwood with tiny louvred panels stood against the wall opposite the bed. Set in the middle of these was a dressing-table made of ebony. A crystal necklace hung over the supporting strut of the oval mirror. One day, rummaging in the tiny drawers, Margot found the rim of a cameo brooch with the cameo missing, an unopened cigar, several small rouge boxes and old lipsticks.

Shallow-Grave reclined, smoking the cigar. Margot fastened the crystal necklace round her mistress's neck and delicately rubbed a little rouge in her cheeks, then, with increasing confidence, applied some lipstick until Shallow-Grave began to look like a magnificent carnival queen from Rio.

"Soon we shall go to Brazil. On a Thursday," said Shallow-Grave. Margot nodded solemnly. The idea of Shallow-Grave as a queen pleased her mightily. She began to make extraordinary head-dresses, temporary by their nature, of paw-paw skin and avocado peel and red and yellow peppers, which she glued together with astonishing dexterity, before placing them on her beloved's head. Then she would hold up a silver-backed hand-mirror for Shallow-Grave to admire the result.

When the house was quiet, Margot slipped out and sorted out new clothing for them both. In the organised maelstrom of the house, no one really noticed the vanishing articles, or if they did, they relied on the fact that whatever vanished usually re-appeared later, that there was a floating sequence of possessions, a dance of objects and articles around the house.

One night while she was exploring, Margot went silently to the top floor where she discovered and pocketed a little bottle of perfume, some amber ear-rings, and two combs. She procured a tablet of green-apple soap, some shampoo, a box of pale face powder and some brightly coloured plastic hair rollers. Becoming increasingly bold, the devoted servant took to exploring parts of the house she had never seen. She went silently, her heart thudding, through the large rooms where swimming patterns of moonlight shifted across the shining wooden floors. On one of her nocturnal outings, she discovered the gallery.

The gallery had once been used for dances. Slender columns linked by a tracery of fretwork supported a ceiling with a painted cupola. Margot glided through. The massive oak sideboard groaned with the weight of silver platters, dusty and unpolished. Ornately carved wooden footstools were scattered around and unvarnished wooden plant-holders had been placed at intervals against the walls. On a marble-topped table stood a glass tray and on the tray sat soft, transparent, miniature purple-and-orange balls of gelatine, some round, some bell-shaped, and some in the shape of fish, full of tiny globules of scented oil. She sniffed the faint, intriguing odours and then pocketed them for her mistress who loved all sorts of perfumes and scents.

Near the door was a large costume box. From the box she pulled out a long red velvet cloak, coronets and tiaras, lorgnettes, pantaloons and all the other paraphernalia of theatre. As she had anticipated, when she returned to their room Shallow-Grave was delighted with these. Margot wanted to dress her in the velvet cloak, but Shallow-Grave dressed herself in a straw hat and black silk T-shirt, crimson boxer shorts, and then performed karate figures in slow motion in front of the mirror.

Later she allowed Margot to drape the cloak around her and serve her food from the china Staffordshire plates she had found, richly coloured with pink, black-edged flowers, decorated with deep-blue and apple-green leaves.

Despite the exhausting nature of her vocational servitude, when she slept at night, Margot breathed peacefully, as if at last she had found a consoling mother.

By now Margot had come to love these night-wanderings. She discovered that the door panels leading to the gallery were painted with scenes of lakes surrounded by dark, tropical vegetation. Downstairs in another part of the house, she found an unoccupied bedroom and lay for a while on the canopied bed, feeling as if the mosquito net was the fine sail of a ship, a gauze of voyaging dreams, and she was a queen from Egypt. She examined the carvings on the legs of the chairs. She explored every nook and cranny of the building.

During the daytime, in their sequestered room, Margot and Shallow-Grave heard all sorts of fragments of life and snatched conversation from the rest of the house.

They heard Adèle the housekeeper panting up the stairs to tell Rita Jenkins, "I gat de videos, Mistress Jenkins. I gat *King Kong, Return of the Dragon, White Nights,* and *Kiss of the Spider Woman.*"

And they heard Armand Jenkins on the phone, trying to reassure his daughter in Canada.

"Of course I want to protect the environment, honey. I care about it just as much as you do." And then they heard him hang up and laugh with a colleague. "Hell, if she only knew. I daren't tell her I'm flying off to the Brazilian border on Thursday to inspect the possibility of a new site near Kato where we'll cause twice as much damage."

Sometimes the sweet voice and American rhythms of Stevie Wonder filled the house with "Part-time Paradise."

And so it was not surprising that both Margot, whose hearing had fully recovered, and Shallow-Grave overheard the telephone ringing in the Jenkinses' bedroom in the early hours of one August morning.

Armand Jenkins fumbled to reach the noisy instrument

in the dark. Three minutes later he was fully awake, trying to absorb the implications of what he was hearing.

The tailings pond of the mine at Omai—a huge pit into which were piped cyanide liquids, other chemicals, and mill wastes—had developed cracks on two sides, two hundred metres across and six metres deep. Three and a half million cubic metres, over three hundred million gallons of dangerous toxic waste were cascading into the Omai River and then rushing in a massive plume down the country's main waterway, the River Essequibo.

Armand Jenkins nearly wet himself with fright. It was possible to conceal most mishaps and leakages at the mine site from the public and the authorities. Omai was far off in the bush. The government could not police it. Normally they could get up to anything. But this news would be impossible to hide.

He switched on the light and swung into action in his nightshirt. Despite the activity around her, Rita Jenkins lay asleep like a beached dolphin. His voice, magnified by panic, was carried upstairs to the house-guests, of whose presence he remained blissfully ignorant, as he phoned the company chairman in Canada.

"We have a major disaster here. I'll cover it up as much as I can, but for god's sake send down the mining engineers who dealt with the company's same problem in South Carolina. Pronto. And I mean pronto as hell," he yelled down the phone. Rita stirred in her sleep.

Blinking in real panic this time, Armand argued over the

phone that, much as he would like to, he could not keep such a massive disaster from the government of Guyana. He had tried that ploy earlier in the year, withholding news of an unauthorised discharge of cyanide for six days. It had not gone down well. He hung up and went and poured himself a neat rum from the cabinet before phoning Cambior's publicity department.

"There's been a catastrophe," he shouted down the phone.

"You mean an unfortunate accident," snapped the public relations man in Montreal, who objected to being woken so early.

"Millions of gallons of cyanide waste is pouring into the main river here."

"You mean there's been a spill. Some seepage." Even as he came to full consciousness, the yawning man in Montreal tried to instruct Armand in the techniques of damage limitation. "Just make sure you control, as far as possible, what is said in the papers. We will put out statements here to mollify the shareholders. If there are any commissions of enquiry, try and ensure that lawyers and businessmen sympathetic to us are on board. Oh yes, and try and plug that leak." The man hung up.

Armand took a deep breath and rang the local newspapers.

A sleepy sub-editor took down the news and perked up as he did so. A big story. Nothing much had happened since Shallow-Grave's escape and they had drawn a complete blank on that. She had just vanished. With some satisfaction, he changed the headline which had been going to read "A hundred and twenty-nine days to Christmas" and wrote "Omai mine seepage."

Margot noticed that her beloved had started to droop. Shallow-Grave said it was merely because she needed to go for a swim. But the day after they overheard Armand on the telephone, her hair lost its healthy spring and her body broke out in a riot of sores that gathered in groups, sent out messengers, erupted in angry outbursts, opened their mouths and yelled. A revolution broke out all over her skin. Margot was horrified. Shallow-Grave explained that a quiet, lengthy bathe in the sea or river would do the trick. She also pointed out that it was time for them to leave the house and head for Brazil. They decided it would be safe to leave and fixed next Thursday for their departure.

Adèle, the Jenkinses' housekeeper, was a stout, down-to-earth woman who came from a practical family. Her sister Mary lived at Bartica, downriver from Omai. Mary arrived to stay with Adèle for a few days until the worst of the poison had passed by and the river had had a chance to clean itself. Hundreds of dead fish had been found. The government had organised for doctors to take hair samples from the Amerindian villagers who lived in scattered communities along the banks, to see if any toxic deposits were detectable. Somehow the samples had been lost on the way back. The Amerindians complained of itching and burning of the skin and blistered mouths. They were too poor to take on the Omai company. In fact, they had no idea of the wealth of the Gold Star people. Later, a few of them were given a handful of dollars for the ruin of their lands and livelihoods, paltry compensation that left the chairman and the board laughing behind their hands in wonder at how they had got away with it.

Adèle listened uneasily to what her sister was saying. It was not like Mary to be superstitious in any way, but now she was talking about sightings of a boat lit with candles that had been seen moving upriver through the choppy waters of the Essequibo. It was sinking near to water-level with the weight of eleven women seated round a magnificent African woman in a blue dress trimmed with red. Each acolyte held a flickering candle and they were singing, laughing, and chattering around the handsome woman who leaned back in the bows of the boat, trailing her hand in the water.

Having played down the Omai disaster as much as possible, Armand Jenkins said good-bye to a grumpy Rita and flew south to the border town of Lethem to await the small private plane that would fly him on to Kato, the place chosen for the next mining operation. He stood outside the guest-house where he had been obliged to stay overnight in the miserable heat of a stifling cubicle and bleakly surveyed the orange dirt track ahead of him. It opened on to a slightly broader clay road. His skin itched and he wondered if there had been bugs in the guest-house. He surveyed the dismally small adobe houses that stood on either side of the road and one or two half-built concrete ones. He decided to go for a walk. His private plane would not arrive until two in the afternoon.

It had taken three days for the engineers to stem the poisoned torrent from Omai. Armand had done his best to dismiss worries and allay government fears. He had assured them that the mighty river would cleanse itself. What he had not told them was that the toxic cocktail of heavy metals, chemically bound with cyanide, tends to enter the marine environment and latch on to micro-organisms. Arsenic, copper, cadmium, lead, mercury become more poisonous over time. These heavy metals are ingested by fish and invertebrates and then bio-magnify and bio-accumulate. They travel through the food chain and end up in the human consumer.

Armand mopped his face with a handkerchief. He walked past the small houses which seemed deserted apart from a few fowls scratching round. He had done his best for the company. He thought he would take a walk by the creek at the back of the main store of the tiny town. It might be cooler there.

Coming down the road towards him was the figure of a tall black woman who, even to Armand, looked out of place. Silhouetted against the blue sky, she picked her way along the road in high-heeled shoes that made her stumble every now and then. Each time that happened, she paused and stared aggressively up at the huge sky as if to defy savannah country. The frilly pink nylon housecoat that floated over a too-tight shiny green skirt, plus the fact that her head was a multi-coloured bouquet of plastic curlers, made her look like a fugitive from a hair-dressing salon. To one ear she held a small portable radio from which Armand could only hear a buzz. But she must have been able to detect music because she was singing in a melodious voice snatches of "Your Cheating Heart." She nodded flirtatiously at Armand before turning abruptly and teetering down the slope to one of the unfinished concrete houses, where she ducked into the doorway and disappeared.

Armand bought himself a beer at the shop and took it with him as he turned down by a bridge at the back of the store and walked along the side of the creek. After about half an hour's scrambling along the wooded banks, he came to a dead tree that had half fallen in the water, its bare branches sticking up like arthritic fingers. He sat astride the trunk where it leaned out over the water, remembering the days of his boyhood in Canada when he used to go fishing in the Great Lakes. He finished off his beer and threw the can in the water.

The sound of a woman singing floated towards him. At the same time, Armand saw the woman that he had encountered earlier. She was naked, dipping herself underwater and standing up. Even in the water, she looked enormous. The breasts of this crooning giantess swung in front of her as she rose from the creek and began to wade towards him, the visible parts of her body shining and gleaming, spangled with drops of water. She did not seem to have seen him sitting astride the tree.

Embarrassed at the sight, Armand remained stock still, hoping she would not notice him. A line of red ants had made its way along the branch where he sat. All at once they made their way up his trouser leg and started to bite his genitals with a fury. Unable to contain himself and with an exclamation of pain, Armand wriggled and slipped off the branch into the waters of the creek. He came up sputtering. There was no sign of the woman. The singing had stopped.

He was looking around once more when he felt a crashing blow to the head. Dazed and sickened, he stumbled forward in the water. Just before he went under, another violent blow rendered him unconscious. Margot stood on the bank with a paddle in her hand, panting with the effort of the blows. Shallow-Grave waded forward and put her hands round Armand's neck. She pulled at the weighty body until it faced upwards, still with the head underwater, and she squeezed her two massive thumbs down on the windpipe, holding the head under until there were no more bubbles.

Still humming, Shallow-Grave pulled the body to the side of the creek. Then she set about scraping at the earth with Margot's paddle to make one of the hollows in the ground that were her trademark and namesake. The two women did not exchange a word. Margot helped, bending her brawny shoulders to dig and scrape as best she could, gazing at her beloved mistress with undisguised admiration as she dragged the body towards the depression in the ground and covered it lightly with earth and leaves.

Hardly anyone witnessed the two women departing for Brazil. The shorter of the two held a red-and-blue umbrella over the taller one and would hurry to execute the most menial request. They took the boat across the Takatu, the larger woman holding on to her straw hat against the Rupununi winds. At Bonfim, few people paid attention to Margot and Shallow-Grave waiting at the side of the road for the bus to Boa Vista. Eventually it arrived covered in white dust and they squeezed themselves on board, in between passengers with live chickens in bags and sacks of provisions.

The last that was heard of them was a report from Boa Vista. They had taken a small room over an electrical goods store in a street near the market that smelled of goat-dung, dried fish, sarsaparilla, and turtle-egg oil as well as the steam of washing. Margot had purchased a tin tub which she carried home on her head and had been seen scouring the market for the herbs to make the *"banho de cheiro."* The blue bath, as she called it.

On their first night in Brazil, Shallow-Grave luxuriated in the hip bath, blue waters lapping at the sides, that Margot had prepared with rue, rosemary, basil, rose-mallow, white-mallow, marjoram, and broom-weed. The oily leaves of rue, both stimulant and narcotic, gave the water its blue colour. A strong smell, bitter and exhilarating, rose up with the steam from the bath, pouring through the holes in the roof and scenting the whole neighbourhood, bewitching it into an unusual and welcome tranquillity.

The aroma, combined with the melodious voice that mingled with the steam and issued from the scabby window on that hypnotically warm evening, stuck in the memories of local people. It was an evening when peace unexpectedly burst over the poorest quarter of Boa Vista. Quarrelsome couples were soothed, fractious babies stopped screaming, shopkeepers refrained from beating the children who begged from their customers. The dwarf woman who washed laundry with manly vigour in the stinking alley outside the electrical goods store joined in the singing as she scrubbed clothes on the dolly-board.

Margot took a chipped enamel bowl with roses on it and poured the waters between the glistening breasts of her mistress as tenderly as if she were watering a transplanted cucumber. After the bath, Margot gave her a quick rub down with bay rum. That, combined with the blue bath, was supposed to ward off evil-doers.

Most extraordinary of all, the butcher, the meanest man in Boa Vista, smiled and threw bones and meat to the endlessly disappointed, starving dogs that hung around his shop. It was the first time that anyone had seen in him a sentiment close to pity.

Rita Jenkins stood in the front room, the telephone in her hand, her bags packed. There had been no sign of Armand for ten weeks. He had disappeared without trace. Tearfully and surrounded by friends on whom she liberally showered small gifts, Rita had waited for news of her husband. Now her shredded nerves demanded that she return to her daughter in Canada. In her worst moments, she feared that he had gone off with another woman. She was on the phone to her lawyer.

"How long would I have to wait before it could be assumed he was dead?" she asked, with an eye to her future circumstances. "That long?" she squeaked in disbelief. The lawyer consoled her with the news that she would receive a huge sum in compensation from the company who would look after her well for the rest of her life. Rita sniffed and hung up.

"Go and call me a taxi to the airport," she ordered Adèle. "Coming back here has done me no good at all at all."

THE OPEN LOT

Jane Weddell took any of several routes from her apartment on West Sixty-fourth Street to the museum on West Seventy-seventh, depending. Her path was determined by a pattern of complexity outside her thought, the result not solely of her emotional state but also of her unconscious desire, say, to avoid a wind blowing black grit down Columbus Avenue on the morning when she was wearing a new blouse for the first time. Or she gave in to whim, following a path defined by successive flights of pigeons, a path that might lead her east down Seventy-third Street to the park instead of across on Seventy-fifth or Sixty-eighth.

The pattern of her traverses from one day to the next gave her a sense of the vastness in which she lived; she was aware not only of the surface of each street but, simultaneously, of the tunneling below, which carried water mains and tree roots, like the meandering chambers of gophers. And ranging above, she knew without having to look, were tiers upon tiers of human life, the joy and anger and curiosity of creatures like herself.

She arrived by one or another of her footpaths—she imagined them, lying awake at night, like a *rete mirabile,* a tracery over the concrete, the tar, and the stone—at a room on the second floor of the Museum of Natural History, a vaulted, well-lit space in which she worked six or seven hours a day, preparing fossils of marine organisms from the Cambrian period and the Precambrian era. It was her gift to discern in the bits of rock placed before her lines of such subtlety that no one who beheld her excisions could quite believe what she had done. Under the bold, piercing glass of a microscope, working first with the right hand and then, when the muscles in that hand lost their strength, the left, she removed clay and sand and silt, grain by grain, her eyes focused on suggestions indescribably ambivalent. When she finished and set the pieces apart, one saw in stone a creature so complete, even to the airiness of its antennae, that it rivaled something living.

From an inchoate maze of creatures alive in the early Paleozoic, she released animal after animal, turned them loose for others to brood over. And from these creatures the systematists cantilevered names, a precarious litany; it was hard to believe that among things so trenchant, despite their silence, names so bloodless would adhere. What was certain was that from a piece of stone in which a creature *might* reside—guessing simply from the way the light broke on its surface—Jane Weddell would pry an animal wild as a swamp night.

The shadow across Jane Weddell's life did not come from living alone, a condition that offered her a peace she esteemed like fresh water; nor being patronized for her great gift by people who avoided her company. It was thrown by the geometry of a life her professional colleagues implied was finally innocuous. No one, perhaps no one in the world, could make the essential pieces of the first puzzle of Earthly life so apparent. But in the eyes of her associates she wandered thoughtlessly outside any orthodoxy in discussing fossils. She strayed from recognized subdivisions of geological time, so people had trouble agreeing on the value of her ideas. Many tried to give meaning to what she did; but because she would neither insist upon nor defend any one theoretical basis for her thought she was ultimately regarded as a technician only. The pattern in her work, what propelled her to the next thing and then the next, was the joy of revelation. She saw no greater purpose in life than to reveal and behold.

What Jane Weddell rendered was conveyed solemnly from the room in which she worked by people who behaved as though they bore off brittle sheaves of IV dynasty papyrus. In adjoining rooms, each creature was photographed, matched to a technical description she provided, inventoried, and given space in a protective case.

Frequently, her exacting descriptions were marked for the attention of one of several researchers who, from this alien menagerie, sought to fathom an ecology of early sea floors. Jane Weddell's memory for any particular fossil was thorough and unconfused; and she understood how the details in this complex, ramulose array of images were related through extraordinary subtleties of shape—but she was rarely consulted. Systematists might ponder at their computer screens for weeks looking for ecological relationships Jane Weddell could have articulated in a moment, if anyone had conveyed to her how they anticipated fitting everything—even these most rarefied forms of early life—together.

She listened politely to urgings that she concentrate on figuring out taxonomic sequences, or that she stick, say, to the Middle Silurian for a while; but she didn't follow through. She hoped, instead, someone might ask what the difference was between two trilobites of the same species where one had been extricated from its matrix with the music of Bach in her ears, the other with Haydn. She wanted to say that there were differences; for her, the precision the systematists sought in their genealogies, even with a foundation as exquisite as the one she provided, was a phantom, a seduction.

In an empty lot on West Seventy-fifth—one that had been cleared of its building and then abandoned to grow up in weeds, feral grasses and ailanthus trees—Jane Weddell occasionally saw phantoms. It was a peripheral sensation, not anything viewed directly but only glimpsed, like a single bird, high up, disappearing between two buildings. The existence of the lot exerted a pressure upon her, like a wind growing imperceptibly but steadily more forceful.

The lot was separated from the sidewalk by a gateless, chain-link fence and shadowed east and west by windowless walls of brick. To the north it was closed off by a high, gray-board fence. One ailanthus, in the far western corner, shaded several hundred square feet. In spring, the grasses grew waist high and among the tall and running weeds purple aster, small white daisy fleabane, and yellow coltsfoot bloomed. In winter the lot fell comatose, exposing a soil of brushed brick and cement powder where shards of glass glinted beside matchbook covers and aluminum cans and where rainwater beaded up on cigarette packs.

Jane Weddell found the lot alluring. One evening when she was walking back late from the museum she saw a small creature run out through the fence and beneath a parked car. She watched motionless for many minutes; then movement on the lip of a trash barrel halfway down the block drew her eye. It was the same animal, discarding some odd bit of debris and falling back into shadow again.

It disturbed Jane Weddell's sense of grace and proportion to be drawn any more to one place than another; she resisted the desire to pass by the lot more frequently once it began to occupy her waking mind. But her sense of perception now grew more acute as she drew near, prepared to catch the faintest signal; and her peripheral awareness intensified. She took in the sky, the shudder of the street beneath her feet, the roll and ruffle of the stout limbs of a London plane tree nearby. To perceive the lot clearly, she believed, she must gain a sense of the whole pattern of which it was a part, taking in even passing cars, the smell of garbage cans, the shriek of schoolchildren.

The lot slowly changed. Through the weeks of spring, and while summer grasses rose up vigorously, bits of broken pipe, a length of coaxial cable, coffee containers, pills of gum foil, a strip of insulation—all this vanished. When Jane Weddell pressed her eyes to the fence now and looked down between the flowering weeds she saw an earth dark as loam.

Cabot Gunther rapped sharply on the translucent glass of Jane Weddell's studio door, a sound that announced he was about to, not might he, enter.

"Jane—there you are, busy in your very perfection."

She regarded him, smiling, wordless, not eager to put him at ease. He walked up close and leaned over her body to see what she was working on.

"Some of the Ediacaran fauna, yes?"

"Yes. They are remarkable, aren't they?" she answered, putting her eyes back to the microscope.

"Jane, I've a difficult thing to convey to you, which is why I've come down here instead of asking you to see me."

She turned to look at him. He found her composure annoying.

"The board met last night, to thrash out the budget. You're still on, I saw to that, but the feeling overall, is that this field"—here he indicated the stone before her—"is drying up, compared to others. The long and short of it is, you've created enough material for us. And since you actually take directions from other people—which periods to focus on, what to look for, and so on—and you yourself are not publishing, the board felt you'd see why we had to cut you back, to four days a week.

"Now, of course, you can still come in whenever you wish—and this will continue to be your office and no one else's—but I can only pay you now for four days a week. That would come out to your annual salary less two months."

She ran the tips of her fingers lightly over her lips but did not say anything.

"I'm sorry. You know it's the ebb and flow of money, Jane, whatever's new, hot. We've covered this before. You could write your own ticket if you'd only publish something, write more than notes, detailed descriptions, if you'd tackle the real meaning of these things, present us with phylogenies and ecologies."

"Would it be possible—"

"Benefits? The benefits package, all that—pension? Unchanged."

"Would you mind if I just went on the same way but took two months off without pay?"

"No, it can't work that way. I have to reduce *each* paycheck twenty percent. You'd in effect be taking two months off with eighty percent of salary. Too much paid vacation, is what it would look like."

She folded her hands under her chin and nodded in polite, wry indignation.

"Don't pout, Jane. It doesn't become you," he said.

"I'm not pouting, Cabe. I'm doing a sort of mathematics. In a few moments it will all seem possible." She smiled at him. "Thank you."

"Make up whatever schedule you want for a week. I'll make the adjustments in the payroll, you can handle the hours, the vacation time, however you want."

He nodded curtly, affirming their agreement, and backed out the door, which he closed gently.

Later that summer, Jane Weddell started a notebook about the lot. She worked evening after evening, divesting her memory of all it held of this place from the afternoon she first saw it two years before; a few weeks after the building had been torn down. The more she demanded of her memory, the more it gave. The first notebook of two hundred pages gave way to a second, and she became aware in her notes of a pattern of replacement, of restored relationships. The incremental change was stunningly confirmed for her the morning she saw a black bear standing in the lot. She could not tell if it was male or female. It was broadside to her in the tall grass, chewing a white tuber. It lifted its head to the air for a scent, or perhaps it was only bothered by grass tickling its chin. She watched until it ambled on toward the gray fence at the back, which it appeared to wander through.

For the first time Jane Weddell decided to change her routing to and from the museum, even though by no longer walking certain streets regularly she knew she would begin to lose her sense of them. She wanted to know more about the open lot. She thought of it as a place she'd been searching for, a choice she was finally making, with which she was immediately at ease. The lot became a sort of companion, like friends she went to dinner with. She didn't press the acquaintance, any more than she did those of her friends. Only occasionally did she pause before the lot and stare for long minutes into its light and shadows. Early in the fall she saw a herd of deer, four does browsing and seeming to take no notice of her. That same morning she didn't notice until she was leaving a switching trail, a tawny panther hunkered in the tawny grass.

Winter came, but the grasses and wildflowers in the lot did not die back as they had the winter before. Every time Jane Weddell passed she would see animals. Even on the rawest days, when wind drove a dry, cold wall of air against her or when sleet fell, she would see foxes bounding. Flocks of chickadees. Sometimes she imagined she could hear a distant river. Other times she saw birds migrating overhead, through the buildings. The lot comforted her, and she puzzled over how she might return the comfort.

When winter was at its steadiest, in January, she went to Aruba with her sister's children. When she came back she saw instantly, the moment she turned the corner at Seventy-seventh Street, that it was gone.

She walked up the block slowly, wondering why she had not done something, whatever that might have been. A construction portico had been erected over the sidewalk. The chain-link fence was now woven with metal slats. She peered through a crevice where a fence post abutted the adjacent building. The lot was not there. A deep excavation faced her. Strands of twisted wire and pipe protruded from the pit's earthen walls. Fresh brick sat foursquare on pallets. Two crane buckets sat crookedly on the ground, half filled with rock and debris.

Jane Weddell stood before two plywood doors padlocked askew at the center of the fence and saw between their edges ten or twelve pigeons, drinking from a throw of rain puddles in the pit. Two workmen arrived in a red and silver pickup. One eyed her accusingly, warning her, as though she were a thief. She left. On the way to the museum she remembered a tray of samples she had set aside years before, rocks so vaguely fossiliferous even she was not sure anything could be drawn from them. So much of the fauna that existed on Earth between Ediacaran fauna in the Precambrian and the first hard-shelled creatures of Cambrian seas was too soft bodied to have left its trace. These rocks were of the right age, she knew, to have included some of these small beasts, and as she climbed the stairs to her studio she knew she was going to extract them, find them if they were in there. More than anything she wanted to coax these ghosts from their tombs, to array them adamantine and gleaming like diamonds below her windows, in shafts of sunlight falling over the city and piercing the thick walls of granite that surrounded her.

FRANCINE PROSE

EVERYTHING IS ABOUT ANIMALS

Her lover is a biologist, a specialist in animal relocation. When the ecologically conscious want to build in a wildlife area, he is called in to move the animal populations and accustom them to their new home.

It took her some time to believe that such a job really existed. Or rather, she believed him until the first time he went away on assignment; then she worried that he had made it all up to escape her. It seemed inconceivable that men who constructed new factories and extended the edges of cities should spend so much money on nature. She could understand why the developers of a new ski resort might worry about displaced resentful bears, but why would a lumber company feel so solicitous about elk?

For comfort, she thought: How could anyone make all that up? Besides, the details of his life added up. He knew every animal language, every bird call, the moony lowing of bison, the high-pitched, complex rattling of hyenas. She loved hearing, but not watching, this; she was embarrassed by the comical ways he had to screw up his face to make these sounds. But often, at night, she'd ask him to do mourning doves or owls, and though it was already dark, she'd close her eyes and imagine her bedroom was a forest. Also she loves making love with him; she feels that watching animals mate has taught him something about men and women—nothing specific, really, but something she has no language for and so cannot describe.

What finally convinced her was nothing he did or said, nor the stories he told, nor the nature photos he showed her, but the charity ball he took her to, at which one hundred beautiful rich women signed pledges to never wear fur coats again. These women all knew him and spoke to him in hushed reverential tones; he smiled and lowered his handsome head toward their mouths. Then she realized that it wasn't the city planners or the corporate heads who were behind this, but the wives of the city planners and corporate heads. And now his stories made sense, made even more sense when he told her: these women would do things for animals, work and care for animals in ways they would never work or care for their fellow men. He is often hired to make sure animals get enough to eat in countries where people are starving.

She has learned to rely on him to make sense of the world. When they watch TV news, he tells her which criminals are innocent, which are guilty, and though his perceptions don't always match hers, she accepts his because she knows he reads deeper signs: lip curls, teeth baring, postures, blinks. She moves to the country, learns to live in the country—for the beauty and quiet, she says, but really to be more like the creatures he so admires. When he is with her, she thinks that this is the right way to live; at other times, she is more aware of the long commute to work.

She too is a scientist—a lab assistant, really. Her boss is a Korean biochemist who believes in the chemical nature of mental illness and gets grants to do elaborate analyses of the blood, sweat, and urine of schizophrenics. The other technicians are friendly, talkative women, mostly from exotic lands; at Friday lunch they have spectacular international pot-lucks. Ordinarily she likes her job, but when her lover is away, she makes frequent mistakes; the experiments require precise timing, and his absence distorts her sense of time. She has to concentrate on the clock, which only reminds her of how long until he comes home. Not that she knows. There is never any telling how long a herd of caribou, say, might take to accept their new grazing lands. She can't help being impatient and ashamed of her impatience, thinking of the animals, thinking: Hurry up and eat.

Also, there is this: to get to her lab, she has to walk down a long corridor past the animal research stations. The smell and the noise—the howls, the perpetual barking behind closed doors—are unspeakable. Usually she can steel herself and go deaf. But when he is gone she feels unworthy of him for not rushing in and throwing open the cages and letting the dogs and cats and rabbits run wild. She fears that her not doing this will undo all the points she imagines herself earning for having put in a garden.

Being with him has made her conscious of resources, of taking advantage. Partly for this, and partly to convince herself there were reasons to move to the country, she has planted a garden. Last year they did this together, but gardening alone is a bore. Now, just to make sure the sun and the smell of the earth don't trick her into happiness, she takes her ghetto blaster out for company and to drown out the sound of the breeze. She plays it loud, glad she lives in a place where there's no one around to hear. People used to talk about rock music killing plants, but her tomatoes do fine; they have grown two feet tall when the deer come in and eat everything. By August the deer are so tame you can yell at them, and they will just stand there looking.

For two months she has been waiting for him to come back from Puerto Rico, where a new factory is displacing a colony of monkeys. The factory will make compact discs. Right from the start, this job irritated him. He said: CDs will never catch on. Leave the monkeys alone; in two years they can have the factory. She pictured monkeys perched on jungle ruins, sailing leftover CDs through the air like frisbees, like silver and rainbow UFOs catching the tropical light. But the company doesn't see it this way, and now the charity is paying him to move the monkeys deeper into the jungle's shrinking heart.

She has not heard from him since he got there. Mostly his jobs are like this—miles from a telephone, mail that takes three weeks to come. He says: Month-old mail is worse than no mail. He'd rather get no letters, would rather not write what will probably not be true by the time it arrives. She thinks this is a little harsh. She would take any mail over no mail, but defers to him in this, and doesn't mention it to her lab technician friends with whom—when she stays in town after work for a movie or a fireworks display—she is trying to have a normal summer. When they ask after him, she smiles and shrugs, meaning, what can you say about someone who'd spend half a summer with monkeys? If she confessed that she never hears from him, they would point out that not writing at all isn't logical, as if she should have just told him that, as if they didn't know how rarely the logical thing is what you do. The Indians and Filipinos all have unhelpful stories of husbands who went off and started second families somewhere else. She knows he will call when he gets to San Juan, and that is, in fact, what happens.

By now she is used to his homecomings, and can get through them if she remembers not to expect any more than this: a certain distance, forgetfulness—that is, he seems to forget who she is and treats her with the dutiful politeness he must have shown whoever sat beside him on the plane ride home. She thinks they should hire an expert to repatriate *him;* but really, she is that expert. She knows what to cook: simple meals, no meat for a while. She could write a cookbook for women whose lovers have lived exclusively among animals. She knows to wait a day for each week he's been gone before thinking he doesn't love her, but even so, even knowing this, she'll still think he doesn't love her, and then *she* will forget, forget what grace she has, drop things in the kitchen, forget where the holes in the lawn are, and trip and fall.

She expects this, she is prepared for it, but not for the man who gets out of his car and walks up her drive after two months in Puerto Rico. Something about him is different, he has lost weight. His body makes a funny angle with the ground, forcing her to see pictures she'd rather not imagine: him hunkering, swinging his arms, screeching monkey talk about food. This is not how she wants to think about him, not ever, and especially not now, as he holds her, a little stiffly, so that she feels silly for hugging him, sees it anthropologically, really no different from jumping and clacking her teeth. Soon he lets her go, making such an effort to look into her eyes that she cannot look back, but only at his hands, hovering disappointedly in the air near her arms.

She offers him a beer but he doesn't want beer. Wine? He refuses. He doesn't want water, doesn't want juice. He isn't hungry. Banana? she says, holding up a bunch. That's not funny, he says, and heads out to the garden before she can warn him that the deer have eaten everything. Soup boils on the stove, she has to turn it down, has to taste it, has to splash soup on her shirt, rub soap in the stain, put water on it, change her shirt. Already she knows to watch for holes in the lawn, so she is tiptoeing, creeping up on him, and so is witness to the most extraordinary sight. Not six feet from him, a doe is grazing what's left of the pepper plants.

He will not eat dinner. He says he ate on the plane, ate something at his apartment. But what could have lasted in his apartment for two months? She has made him fresh corn chowder, broiled swordfish, red potatoes, sliced cucumbers with soy sauce and sesame oil, but she can't eat much either. She does dishes, they go for a walk up the road. By now he has been in her house six hours. Then they go to bed. He keeps turning her, he will only make love to her from behind. She knows not to turn and look, it would be awful to see how surprised he'd be to see her face. And anyway, she prefers it this way: he can't see she is crying. Later they lie there, not talking. She thinks he is totally gone, gone crazy, or worse, is going to tell her he's fallen in love with a monkey.

After a while he says he is sorry. He lies on his back and tells the ceiling that he is having a very bad time. He says what he found in Puerto Rico were forty or fifty monkeys, mostly adults—strong, unpredictable, destructive. First they harassed, then actually attacked a couple of workers building the plant, a couple of monkeys were shot before he was called in. They moved the monkeys in cages on pickup trucks: it was like the aftermath of a war, like some Hollywood epic retreat scene, complete with the bloody bandages. He says everyone knows stories about animal populations that just didn't make it, didn't adapt. He had never seen this himself, but there was something about these monkeys that made him think of it right away.

At first he kept them in cages. He let them watch him gathering food, picking the bananas and breadfruit he then left within their reach. The monkeys picked the bananas up and looked at them and dropped them. They stayed on a kind of hunger strike for a week. Finally he gave up; maybe they needed to gather the food themselves. So he let them out of the cages, but now *he* had to be in a cage, for his own protection. Getting them out, and him in, was a complicated maneuver, but he did it, and still the monkeys wouldn't forage, wouldn't eat.

After two weeks he could see that they'd gotten thinner. *He* began eating like crazy, bananas, bananas, bananas, showing them how it was done, but they knew that. They didn't want it. Another two weeks and the monkeys were very skinny, but there was nothing he could do, no one was going to force-feed them. Hospitalize them? Hook them all up to IVs? He began writing letters—Help, the monkeys are starving—mailing them out with the helicopters that dropped him extra food. And now he could see the monkeys getting dull and slack and sleepy; their fur was beginning to fall out. But maybe they were sneaking something at night, because it all happened so slowly, the whole thing took longer than he could believe.

Toward the end he thought of getting the trucks back and trucking them into the city and letting the monkeys die in the middle of downtown San Juan. But what would that have accomplished, except maybe scaring some children and getting him and the starving monkeys thrown in jail? So he stayed out in the jungle until they died. The children and the old ones went first. It took days, it was awful, bodies everywhere, like some nightmare monkey Jonestown. After he'd buried them all, he went into town. It was in San Juan that he realized he had stopped eating. He didn't—still doesn't—remember when he last ate. When he tries to eat, his throat clenches and he thinks he is going to choke.

Neither of them sleeps all night, though they both pretend. She wonders if monkeys ever pretend to sleep. She thinks of how once, long ago, a lover left her for someone else, a friend, a woman who used to visit them, and how the worst thing was wondering if the best way to win him back was to be more or less like that friend. What she feels now is so similar; she thinks: Should I be more human or more monkey?

In the morning she says she has a favor to ask him. She's read that the best thing to do with the garden would be to turn the ground over now, stockpile manure and lay it on before fall, before the snow. She has arranged with a neighbor to borrow his pickup, and a farmer just down the road has said they can have some manure from his barn. Will he help her while he is here?

She has given this a lot of thought, so it is not nearly as weird as it might seem, asking a lover who's just come home after two months to help you go get cowshit. She has found that chores like this—simple, physically demanding tasks connected unquestionably to survival—seem to do him good when he returns. The quickest recovery he ever made was one winter after he'd been with the elk: she got him to go out and split most of a cord of wood. Plus, this time she can't help hoping that her planning for seasons ahead will make him think well of her, see in her the best of human intelligence and animal instinct combined.

He says that he would be glad to help. He even makes a joke of being back twenty-four hours and already shoveling shit. She sees this as a good sign. She makes a point of how he has old clothes—boots, overalls, a shirt—stored in the front hall closet. Look, she says, your stuff. It takes some restraint not to ask if he's sure he doesn't want breakfast.

They drive to the farm. The farmer shows them where to find the manure. They back the truck up to the barn door and start shoveling. They haven't worked long, a few minutes perhaps, but already this job they are doing together— efficiently, wordlessly—is making her feel more hopeful.

Then he sticks his pitchfork into the pile and exposes a nest of wriggling pink creatures, no bigger than a finger, blind, squirming and squealing in terror. What are they? Newborn mice? Impossibly tiny pigs? Surely he knows, but doesn't say; and suddenly she feels so distant from him that she can't even ask. She thinks she may always remember these creatures and never know what they were. He throws a ragged slab of manure back on top of the nest, gently tamps it down so the animals are covered, then goes out and sits in the truck. In a little while she joins him, he guns the engine, and they leave. She wonders how she will explain this the next time she sees the farmer.

At home she makes coffee. He puts his hands around the cup but doesn't drink. Through the window, she can see the pickup, the few clumps of manure still unloaded in back. Perfect, she thinks. He tells her he can't be with her, can't be with anyone now. He says it isn't fair to her, he is in terrible shape. He means it, he talks without stopping, without leaving her any silences in which to wedge an offer of patience or help. Then he gets in his car and drives off.

She sits quietly for a while, wondering if, and how much, she should worry about him. Starving yourself is serious business. But then she thinks: He won't starve, he'll be all right, he is an expert on survival. This makes her feel slightly worse—does this mean she would rather he go crazy than just not love her? And *this* makes her think she

126

deserves what has happened: she has not loved him unselfishly, or enough.

Now she is sorry she has taken this week off from work. She had imagined them spending it together. She would be better off in the lab, distracted, but she has told her friends at work he is coming home. If she cancels her vacation and goes in, she'll have to talk about him.

The first day of vacation she goes to the store and buys lots of food. After that she stays home. She decides not to call him. Instead she will make a list of things to remember to tell him, things that happen to her. Then she'll have the list if he calls.

At the end of the week he still hasn't called, so she decides to call *him.* She picks up the phone and as she dials, reads the list:

1. A flock of geese flew overhead and she thought it was barking dogs.

2. In the grocery store, she overheard one teenage mother telling another how, the first year after her kid was born, she rented a trailer from an old guy who had put an electronic bug zapper right outside her bedroom window. The purple light and the zapping kept waking up the baby. She kept turning the light off, but the landlord kept sneaking back over and turning it on, and finally they had an argument and he evicted her.

3. After that trip to the grocery store, she stopped going out, and spent the rest of her vacation in bed. She ate in

bed, didn't bathe, watched a lot of TV. Her favorite part of the day was the early morning, before she was fully awake. She would put her head under the covers, where it was warm and smelled of her body, and she breathed in the smell, with its edge of the zoo, a little bit like his smell.

She reads through the list again. She puts down the phone. She thinks: I have nothing to tell him that isn't about animals.

E. L. DOCTOROW

WILLI

One spring day I walked in the meadow behind the barn
and felt rising around me the exhalations of the field, the
moist sweetness of the grasses, and I imagined the earth's
soul lifting to the warmth of the sun and mingling me in
some divine embrace. There was such brilliant conviction
in the colors of the golden hay meadow, the blue sky, that I
could not help laughing. I threw myself down in the grass
and spread my arms. I fell at once into a trance and yet remained incredibly aware, so that whatever I opened my
eyes to look at I did not merely see but felt as its existence.
Such states come naturally to children. I was resonant with
the hum of the universe, I was made indistinguishable from
the world in a great bonding of natural revelation. I saw the
drowse of gnats weaving between the grasses and leaving
infinitesimally fine threads of shimmering net, so highly
textured that the breath of the soil below lifted it in gentle
billows. Minute crawling life on the stalks of hay made

colossal odyssey, journeys of a lifetime, before my eyes. Yet there was no thought of miracle, of the miracle of microscopic sentience. The scale of the universe was not pertinent, and the smallest indications of energy were in proportion to the sun, which lay like an Egyptian eye between the stalks, and lit them as it lights the earth, by halves. The hay had fallen under me so that my own body's outline was patterned on the field, the outspread legs and arms, the fingers, and I was aware of my being as the arbitrary shape of an agency that had chosen to make me in this manner as a means of communicating with me. The very idea of a head and limbs and a body was substantive only as an act of communication, and I felt myself in the prickle of the flattened grass, and the sense of imposition was now enormous, a prodding, a lifting of this part of the world that was for some reason my momentary responsibility, that was giving me possession of itself. And I rose and seemed to ride on the planes of the sun, which I felt in fine striations, alternated with thin lines of the earth's moist essences. And invisibled by my revelation, I reached the barn and examined the face of it, standing with my face in the painted whiteness of its glare as a dog or a cat stands nose to a door until someone comes and lets it out. And I moved along the white barn wall, sidestepping until I came to the window which was a simple square without glass, and could only be felt by the geometrical coolness of its volume of inner air, for it was black within. And there I

stood, as if in the mouth of a vacuum, and felt the insub-
stantial being of the sun meadow pulled past me into the
barn, like a torrential implosion of light into darkness and
life into death, and I myself too disintegrated in that force
and was sucked like the chaff of the field in that roaring.
Yet I stood where I was. And in quite normal spatial relationship with my surroundings felt the sun's quiet warmth
on my back and the coolness of the cool barn on my face.
And the windy universal roar in my ears had narrowed and
refined itself to a recognizable frequency, that of a woman's
pulsating song in the act of love, the gasp and note and gasp
and note of an ecstatic score. I listened. And pressed upon
by the sun, as if it were a hand on the back of my neck, I
moved my face into the portal of the cool darkness, and no
longer blinded by the sunlight, my eyes saw on the straw
and in the dung my mother, denuded, in a pose of utmost
degradation, a body, a reddened headless body, the head
enshrouded in her clothing, everything turned inside out,
as if blown out by the wind, all order, truth, and reason,
and this defiled mama played violently upon and being
made to sing her defilement. How can I describe what I
felt! I felt I deserved to see this! I felt it was my triumph,
but I felt monstrously betrayed. I felt drained suddenly of
the strength to stand. I turned my back and slid down the
wall to a sitting position under the window. My heart in
my chest banged in sickened measure of her cries. I wanted
to kill him, this killer of my mother who was killing her. I

wanted to leap through the window and drive a pitchfork into his back, but I wanted him to be killing her, I wanted him to be killing her for me. I wanted to be him. I lay on the ground, and with my arms over my head and my hands clasped and my ankles locked, I rolled down the slope behind the barn, through the grass and the crop of hay. I flattened the hay like a mechanical cylinder of irrepressible force rolling fast and faster over rocks, through rivulets, across furrows and over hummocks of the uneven imperfect flawed irregular earth, the sun flashing in my closed eyes in diurnal emergency, as if time and the planet had gone out of control. As it has. (I am recalling these things now, a man older than my father when he died, and to whom a woman of my mother's age when all this happened is a young woman barely half my age. What an incredible achievement of fantasy is the scientific mind! We posit an empirical world, yet how can I be here at this desk in this room—and not be here? If memory is a matter of the stimulation of so many cells of the brain, the greater the stimulus—remorse, the recognition of fate—the more powerfully complete becomes the sensation of the memory until there is transfer, as in a time machine, and the memory is in the ontological sense another reality.) Papa, I see you now in the universe of your own making. I walk the polished floorboards of your house and seat myself at your dining table. I feel the tassels of the tablecloth on the tops of my bare knees. The light of the candelabra shines on your smiling mouth of big teeth. I notice the bulge of your neck produced by your shirt collar. Your pink scalp is visible through the close-cropped German-style haircut. I see your head raised in conversation and your white plump hand of consummate gesture making its point to your wife at the other end of the table. Mama is so attentive. The candle flame burns in her eyes and I imagine the fever there, but she is quite calm and seriously engrossed by what you say. Her long neck, very white, is hung with a thin chain from which depends on the darkness of her modest dress a cream-colored cameo, the carved profile of another fine lady of another time. In her neck a soft slow pulse beats. Her small hands are folded and the bones of her wrists emerge from the touch of lace at her cuffs. She is smiling at you in your loving proprietorship, proud of you, pleased to be yours, and the mistress of this house, and the mother of this boy. Of my tutor across the table from me who idly twirls the stem of his wineglass and glances at her, she is barely aware. Her eyes are for her husband. I think now Papa her feelings in this moment are sincere. I know now each moment has its belief and what we call treachery is the belief of each moment, the wish for it to be as it seems to be. It is possible in joy to love the person you have betrayed and to be refreshed in your love for him, it is entirely possible. Love renews all faces and customs and ideals and leaves the bars of the prison shining. But how could a boy know that? I ran to my room and waited for someone to follow me. Whoever dared to enter my room, I would attack—would pummel. I wanted it to be her, I wanted her to come to me, to hug me and to hold my head and kiss me on the lips as she liked to do, I wanted her to make those wordless sounds of comfort as she held me to her when I was hurt or unhappy, and when she did that I would beat her with my fists, beat her to the floor, and see her raise her hands helplessly in terror as I beat her and kicked her and jumped upon her and drove the breath from her body. But it was my tutor who, sometime later, opened the door, looked in with his hand upon the knob, smiled, said a few words, and wished me good night. He closed the door and I heard him walk up the steps to the next floor, where he had his rooms. Ledig was his name. He was a Christian. I had looked but could not find in his face any sign of smugness or leering pride or cruelty. There was nothing coarse about him, nothing that could possibly give me offense. He was barely twenty. I even thought I saw in his eyes a measure of torment. He was habitually melancholic anyway, and during my lessons his mind often wandered and he would gaze out the window and sigh. He was as much a schoolboy as his pupil. So there was every reason to refrain from judgment, to let time pass, to think, to gain understanding. Nobody knew that I knew. I had that choice. But did I? They had made my position intolerable. I was given double vision, the kind that comes with a terrible blow. I found I could not have anything to do with my kind sweet considerate mother. I found I could not bear the gentle pedagogics of my tutor. How, in that rural isolation, could I be expected to go on? I had no friends, I was not permitted to play with the children of the peasants who worked for us. I had only this trinity of Mother and Tutor and Father, this unholy trinity of deception and ignorance who had excommunicated me from my life at the age of thirteen. This of course in the calendar of traditional Judaism is the year a boy enjoys his initiation into manhood.

Meanwhile my father was going about the triumph of his life, running a farm according to the most modern principles of scientific management, astonishing his peasants and angering the other farmers in the region with his success. The sun brought up his crops, the Galician Agricultural Society gave him an award for the quality of his milk, and he lived in the state of abiding satisfaction given to individuals who are more than a match for the life they have chosen for themselves. I had incorporated him into the universe of giant powers that I, a boy, experienced in the changes of the seasons. I watched bulls bred to cows, watched mares foal, I saw life come from the egg and the multiplicative wonders of mudholes and ponds, the jell and slime of life shimmering in gravid expectation. Everywhere I looked, life sprang from something not life, insects unfolded from sacs on the surface of still waters and were instantly on the prowl for their dinner, everything that came into being knew at once what to do and did it unastonished that it was what it was, unimpressed by where it was, the great earth heaving up its bloodied newborns from every pore, every cell, bearing the variousness of itself from every conceivable substance which it contained in itself, sprouting life that flew or waved in the wind or blew from the mountains or stuck to the damp black underside of rocks, or swam or suckled or bellowed or silently separated in two. I placed my father in all of this as the owner and manager. He lived in the universe of giant powers by understanding it and making it serve him, using the daily sun for his crops and breeding what naturally bred, and so I distinguished him in it as the god-eye in the kingdom, the intelligence that brought order and gave everything its value. He loved me and I can still feel my pleasure in making him laugh, and I might not be deceiving myself when I remember the feel on my infant hand of his unshaved cheek, the winy smell of his breath, the tobacco smoke in his thick wavy hair, or his mock-wondering look of foolish happiness during our play together. He had close-set eyes, the color of dark grapes, that opened wide in our games. He would laugh like a horse and show large white teeth. He was a strong man, stocky and powerful—the constitution I inherited—and he had emerged as an orphan from the alleys of cosmopolitan eastern Europe, like Darwin's amphibians from the sea, and made himself a landowner, a husband and father. He was a Jew who spoke no Yiddish and a farmer raised in the city. I was not allowed to play with village children, or to go to their crude schools. We lived alone, isolated on our estate, neither Jew nor Christian, neither friend nor petitioner of the Austro-Hungarians, but in the pride of the self-constructed self. To this day I don't know how he arranged it or what hungering rage had caused him to deny every classification society imposes and to live as an anomaly, tied to no past in a world which, as it happened, had no future. But I am in awe that he did it. Because he stood up in his life he was exposed to the swords of Mongol horsemen, the scythes of peasants in revolution, the lowered brows of monstrous bankers and the cruciform gestures of prelates. His arrogance threatened him with the cumulative power of all of European history which was ready to take his head, nail it to a pole and turn him into one of the scarecrows in his fields, arms held stiffly out toward life. But when the moment came for this transformation, it was accomplished quite easily, by a word from his son. I was the agency of his downfall. Ancestry and myth, culture, history and time were ironically composed in the shape of his own boy.

I watched her for several days. I remembered the rash of passion on her flesh. I was so ashamed of myself that I felt continuously ill, and it was the vaguest, most diffuse nausea, nausea of the blood, nausea of the bone. In bed at night I found it difficult breathing, and terrible waves of fever

broke over me and left me parched in my terror. I couldn't
purge from my mind the image of her overthrown body,
the broad whiteness, her shoed feet in the air; I made her
scream ecstatically every night in my dreams and awoke
one dawn in my own sap. That was the crisis that toppled
me, for in fear of being found out by the maid and by my
mother, for fear of being found out by them all as the
archcriminal of my dreams, I ran to him, I went to him for
absolution, I confessed and put myself at his mercy. Papa, I
said. He was down by the kennels mating a pair of vizslas.
He used this breed to hunt. He had rigged some sort of
harness for the bitch so that she could not bolt, a kind of
pillory, and she was putting up a terrible howl, and though
her tail showed her amenable, she moved her rump away
from the proddings of the erect male, who mounted and
pumped and missed and mounted again and couldn't hold
her still. My father was banging the fist of his right hand
into the palm of his left. Put it to her, he shouted, come on,
get it in there, give it to her. Then the male had success and
the mating began, the female standing there quietly now,
sweat dripping off her chops, an occasional groan escaping
from her. And then the male came, and stood front paws on
her back, his tongue lolling as he panted, and they waited as
dogs do for the detumescence. My father knelt beside them
and soothed them with quiet words. Good dogs, he said,
good dogs. You must guard them at this time, he said to me,
they try to uncouple too early and hurt themselves. Papa, I

said. He turned and looked at me over his shoulder as he knelt beside the dogs, and I saw his happiness, and the glory of him in his workpants tucked into a black pair of riding boots and his shirt open at the collar and the black hair of his chest curled as high as the throat, and I said, Papa, they should be named Mama and Ledig. And then I turned so quickly I do not even remember his face changing, I did not even wait to see if he understood me, I turned and ran, but I am sure of this—he never called after me.

There was a sun room in our house, a kind of conservatory with a glass outer wall and slanted ceiling of green glass framed in steel. It was a very luxurious appointment in that region, and it was my mother's favorite place to be. She had filled it with plants and books, and she liked to lie on a chaise in this room and read and smoke cigarettes. I found her there, as I knew I would, and I gazed at her with wonder and fascination because I knew her fate. She was incredibly beautiful, with her dark hair parted in the center and tied behind her in a bun, and her small hands, and the lovely fullness of her chin, the indications under her chin of some fattening, like a quality of indolence in her character. But a man would not dwell on this as on her neck, so lovely and slim, or the high modestly dressed bosom. A man would not want to see signs of the future. Since she was my mother it had never occurred to me how many years younger she was than my father. He had married her out of the gymnasium; she was the eldest of four daughters and

her parents had been eager to settle her in prosperous welfare, which is what a mature man offers. It is not that the
parents are unaware of the erotic component for the man in
this sort of marriage. They are fully aware of it. Rectitude,
propriety, are always very practical. I gazed at her in wonder and awe. I blushed. What? she said. She put her book
down and smiled and held out her arms. What, Willi, what
is it? I fell into her arms and began to sob and she held me
and my tears wet the dark dress she wore. She held my
head and whispered, What, Willi, what did you do to yourself, poor Willi? Then, aware that my sobs had become
breathless and hysterical, she held me at arm's length—
tears and snot were dribbling from me—and her eyes
widened in genuine alarm.

That night I heard from the bedroom the shocking exciting sounds of her undoing. I have heard such terrible
sounds of blows upon a body in Berlin after the war,
Freikorps hoodlums in the streets attacking whores they
had dragged from the brothel and tearing the clothes from
their bodies and beating them to the cobblestones. I sat up
in bed, hardly able to breathe, terrified, but feeling undeni-
able arousal. Give it to her, I muttered, banging my fist in
my palm. Give it to her. But then I could bear it no longer
and ran into their room and stood between them, lifting
my screaming mother from the bed, holding her in my
arms, shouting at my father to stop, to stop. But he
reached around me and grabbed her hair with one hand

and punched her face with the other. I was enraged, I pushed her back and jumped at him, pummeling him, shouting that I would kill him. This was in Galicia in the year 1910. All of it was to be destroyed anyway, even without me.

WOLF AT THE DOOR

The last pink wash of daylight through the den window was no longer enough. Hiram Finch pulled the beaded chain on the green-shaded lamp beside the table and continued writing. His pen had moved fluidly from a rather controlled script to a loose scrawl that was allowing him only a few words per line. He paused, sipped his tea, then filled his cup again from the fat blue pot that had been a gift from an Australian couple who had come through with a sick horse a couple of years ago. He got up, opened the woodstove, and laid the page down on the red-and-orange glowing coals. He watched it catch flame and then closed the door. He heard the quiet steps of his wife approaching from the stairs.

"You need another log on the stove," Carolyn said, sitting down in the overstuffed chair and blowing on a mug of coffee. The aperture of her lips was perfect for playing her flute, which for so many years had lain idle in a drawer somewhere in the house. "I think it's colder in here than it is outside."

Hiram put a couple of small alder logs into the stove and poked at them with the iron, loosening the bark to allow the flames to lick through to the wood.

"I think you should just let it go," Carolyn said.

Hiram nodded and sat back at the table by the window, picked up the pen and tapped it against his corduroy leg. "I suppose that would be the wise and prudent thing to do."

"I suppose."

"This table is getting wobbly," Hiram said, grabbing it by the edge and giving it a small shake.

"You're just going to get all riled up and then they're going to do what they're going to do anyway." She blew on her coffee. "Just follow the path of least resistance for once."

"Just leave me alone. Please."

"Sure thing." Carolyn sipped from her mug.

"Listen, I'm sorry. I didn't mean it like that."

"Okay."

Hiram sighed. "Christ, I just apologized."

"And I said 'okay.' Okay?" Carolyn stood and looked about the room as if trying to remember some undone task. "I'm going upstairs to read for a while."

"All right."

Hiram watched her leave the room. He tossed the pen onto the table and looked out at the lavender-approaching-violet sky. He'd seen a falcon knife through the night out this window earlier, right across the moon like a ghost, and he wanted to see one now. Carolyn was probably right, he should just let it go. He couldn't stop them. The lion was indeed dangerous; any animal like that which wasn't terrified of people was dangerous. It apparently was not the least bit shy like other big cats. It came down to kill a lamb or a couple of chickens every couple of weeks and had nearly scared to death a teenage boy who was tending a fence. Although it was unclear whether the animal was actually interested in him, because in the boy's words it walked by "just as casual as anything." So they were going to kill him or her; no one knew the sex of the cat. They only knew that it killed and was large and wasn't much impressed by human presence. Hiram's irate and raging letter to the county commission wasn't going to stop them from putting a bounty on the lion's head. The crazy veterinarian who lived on the hill might be fine for looking into bovine eyes and studying the stool samples of sheep and horses and dogs, but what did he know about lions?

Hiram heard Carolyn upstairs in the study and felt bad for talking to her the way he had. He got up and climbed the stairs, leaned against the doorjamb, and watched her scanning the books in the case.

"I'm sorry about the way I acted," he said.

"That's okay," she said without looking up from the books.

"You're right about letting it go, you know."

"Whatever."

Hiram watched as she took a book and sat down on the love seat. "I'm going to check the horses." If she did offer a response, Hiram didn't hear her. He went back downstairs and left the house. He crossed the yard to the stables, finding as he entered that the horses were somewhat agitated, stepping back and forth and complaining a little.

"What's wrong, girls?" he said, turning on the lights and looking through the center of the barn and out the back. "What's got you all jittery?" He took the flashlight from the wall by the door and walked across the dirt floor, shining his beam into the corners of the stalls, and petting the noses of his horses. "No food now, silly," he said to his too-fat Appaloosa. He walked out the other side of the barn and shined the light into the corral, sweeping the baked hard ground for any sign, although he knew this was a wasted effort given the condition of the earth and his ineptitude as a tracker.

Hiram recalled when he was seventeen and his father's flock had been attacked by what was thought to be a wolf. Two lambs and two ewes had been torn to pieces and were strewn about the pasture nearest the house. That was the amazing part, that the carnage had been so close. Hiram's father was upset with eight-year-old Carla because she had the sheepdog sleeping with her in the house.

"At least, he would have barked and I would have known something was going on," Hiram's father said. He stood at the fence just outside the back door and looked out across the pasture. "Damn wolf."

"Zöe could have been killed, too," Carla said.

Hiram's father didn't respond. Hiram had been walking about the pasture. The sheep ran from him every time he drew near, still anxious, still bleating crazily. He was on the other side of the fence.

"Dad, I don't think it was wolves," Hiram said.

"And why do you say that?"

"A wolf wouldn't have killed so many animals."

"Wolves, then."

"Wolves don't kill like that. They would kill only the lambs and eat them; they wouldn't leave most of them lying all over the place. I think it was dogs. I think somebody's dogs got loose and went wild."

"You know as well as I do that there's a wolf around. You saw him with your own eyes up on the mountain."

"I think it's dogs." Hiram looked down at Carla and then at the border collie who was scratching her ear with a hind foot. "And I think they would have killed ol' ugly right there if she had been out."

"Zöe's not ugly," Carla said and she knelt to hug the animal around the neck.

Hiram's father was not much taken with the theory. He just muttered something about getting his rifle.

The following day, a fine rain fell and most of the mountain seemed unusually quiet. Hiram sat astride his horse, Jack, a twelve-year-old gelding who behaved as if he were three. He held his father's Weatherby rifle across his lap while he watched his father, who had dismounted and was poking through a pile of animal scat with a stick.

"Looks like dog," Hiram said.

Hiram's father nodded and climbed back into his saddle. "I don't know. Got hair in it."

They rode on up the mountain and Hiram recalled all the stories the Indians told about the wolf and its power and he wanted to believe that the animals were a part of the place, wanted to believe that he was part of the place. His father and mother always laughed at him when he talked about such things, called him "youthful." Hiram didn't know any Indians but he had read a lot about them, especially the Plains Indians, and although he knew that his sources might be questionable, he still wanted to believe them.

"Dad," Hiram said as they topped a ridge. "Can't we just scare the wolf away?"

Hiram's father laughed. "You mean like reason with him?"

"What about getting one of those tranquilizer guns and relocating him?"

Hiram's father shook his head. "Where would we get one of them guns? Besides, we can't afford it. Nah. Anyway, a wolf ain't nothing but a big, evil dog."

147

The caked blood was still flowing slowly from the cuts across the backs of the palomino's hind feet. Hiram let go of the leg and stood away, perspiration dripping from his face. The woman holding the horse's halter stroked his nose and settled him down, making soothing sounds, the kind of sounds one reserves for animals. The horse had gotten tangled in some barbed wire.

"I could just shoot myself," the woman said.

Hiram shrugged. "Accidents happen to animals, too."

"It's my fault though."

"The wounds aren't too bad," Hiram said, coughing into a fist. "The worst part is across his fetlocks. I'm going to give him a shot of antibiotics and leave an iodine solution with you. Just dab it on twice a day. Might sting him a little."

"He's such a big baby," the woman said.

"Yeah, I know. It's because he's a male." Hiram reached into his bag for the antibiotic and syringe. "You can't blame yourself," he said. "What good does that do?" He filled the syringe, stood, and quickly stuck the horse's flank, pressing the plunger in. He saw the woman flinch. "Better him than you." Hiram had known Marjorie Stoval since she and her husband moved down from Colorado Springs six years before. He was used to seeing mainly her during his calls. The last few times Mr. Stoval had been conspicuously absent; the toy sports car that never seemed to go anywhere was now gone. He looked past the horse at the rolling pasture and the steep foothills behind it, ochre and red in the heat of early summer.

"You've got a sweet place here," Hiram said.

Marjorie nodded, stroked the blond horse's neck, pulling his mane with each pass. She seemed lost in thought. She was an attractive, young-looking woman, but Hiram believed from previous conversations that she was about forty-five, although there was not much gray in the dark hair she wore pulled back.

"Well, I guess I'm done." Hiram closed his bag and picked it up, yawned, and as he did, realized that it was a tic of his that surfaced when he was nervous.

"Tired?" Marjorie asked.

"I guess." As they walked back toward Hiram's truck, he said, "Other than the scratches, Cletus looks pretty good."

"My husband left me," Marjorie Stoval said abruptly.

Hiram swallowed and looked beyond his truck at the two-story log house. "Yeah, well, I suppose these things happen."

"He moved in with a young woman over in Eagle Nest. They live in a trailer. Can you imagine that?"

Hiram shook his head. At the truck he put his bag in the bed, pushed forward against the cab wall, cleared his throat, and turned to the woman. "My wife and I are pretty decent company. Why don't we call you and arrange a dinner over at our place?"

Marjorie paused as if considering whether the offer was some kind of mercy dinner, then said, "That sounds nice," in a noncommittal way as she smoothed the hair back from her face.

Carolyn was painting a metal chair set on spread-out newspapers on the front porch. Hiram stopped and looked at her. He reached forward and wet his finger with the blue paint streaked across her forehead.

"I'm glad this stuff is water-based," she said, setting the brush across the open can and standing up straight. She stretched her back and smiled at him.

Hiram smiled back, remembering a time when they would have kissed, a time when he would be gone most of the day and would miss her badly and she would miss him, too. They used to talk a few times during his work day, but not now. Now, he simply came home, Carolyn smiled at him, and he smiled back.

"Anything interesting today?" she asked as she stepped back to scrutinize her work. "I don't know if I really like this blue. What do you think?"

"Blue is blue." Hiram stepped past his wife and into the house, putting his bag on the table just inside the door and walked into the den where he fell into the overstuffed chair in front of the woodstove. He glanced at the coffee table where there was a stack of journals he had been meaning to read, needed to read.

Carolyn came in and sat on the sofa. She was sighing and still stretching her back.

"Is your back all right?" Hiram asked.

"It's just stiff from squatting."

"Would you like me to rub it for you?" he asked, but he didn't really want to do it. He would have liked a back rub, but the offer was not forthcoming from Carolyn. He leaned his head back, briefly studied the ceiling, then closed his eyes.

"Maybe later," she said, her voice sounding far away. "I found a lump on Zack's belly this afternoon." Her voice was closer now. Zack was a one-hundred-twenty-pound mutt Hiram had brought home from the shelter about five years ago. "It's kinda big."

"Where on his belly?"

"Just above his tallywhacker," Carolyn said.

Hiram chuckled at the term. "How big?"

"Golf ball."

"I noticed it a couple of weeks ago. It's an umbilical hernia. I decided to leave it alone. It was about the size of a gumball then."

"Well, it's bigger now."

"I'll fix him up tomorrow. It's going to be a slow day. Yep, I'll just cut the ol' boy open and fix him right up."

Carolyn left the room. Hiram listened as she started to get dinner together in the kitchen. He went to help, the way he helped every night. The accounting firm where Carolyn once worked had folded and she hadn't found a new job. It had been two years and she'd pretty much resigned herself to not finding anything, so she had stopped looking. Hiram didn't care. They had enough money. They didn't do much traveling. But he hated her periodic complaining about being a housewife. He would respond by saying that he didn't think of her as a housewife, but rather a full-time gardener/painter/wrangler/everything else. He'd point out how much money she was saving them by doing what someone else would charge a bundle to do. But she still complained while doing nothing about it. He walked to the kitchen cupboard for the dishes.

"I was over at the Stoval place today," Hiram said. "Did you know that Mr. Stoval just up and left?"

"Really?"

"Mrs. Stoval told me. I guess she doesn't have many people to talk to, being out there all by herself."

"She was lucky you were there, wasn't she?"

Hiram set the plates on the table and looked at Carolyn. "Anyway, I mentioned that we might have her over for dinner."

"How nice."

"What is it with you? If I were talking about Mitch Greeley or old Mrs. Jett, you wouldn't sound like this."

Without looking away from the pasta on the stove, Carolyn said, "I don't guess we'd be having the same conversation about them."

"We don't have to invite her."

Carolyn turned off the flame under the pasta, then drained off the water in the sink before turning to Hiram. "I'm sorry. I'm tightly wound today. I think I'm feeling cooped up or something."

"Want to go out? Drive to town and take in a movie?"

Carolyn shook her head.

"What about an early morning walk up to the falls?"

Carolyn smiled in weak agreement.

An hour after dinner someone rang the bell. Hiram and Carolyn were reading in the den. Hiram was just beginning to nod off; the journal was resting on his lap. Carolyn looked at him as if to say, who could that be? and didn't move. Hiram got up and went to the door, opened it, and found Lewis Fife, all three hundred pounds of him standing on the porch.

"Well, they did it," Lewis Fife said quickly. He was out of breath, panting.

"You didn't walk over here, did you?" Hiram asked.

"Are you crazy? Of course not. I drove, but I took your steps two at a time," Lewis Fife said.

"There's only four steps, Lewis."

"Give me a break, man. I weigh a ton. You try hauling this shit around." He grabbed his stomach and showed it to Hiram. "Are you going to let me in?"

Hiram stepped aside and called back to Carolyn as the big man entered. "It's Lewis."

Carolyn came and stood in the doorway to the den. "Good evening, Lewis," she said.

"Ma'am," Lewis said and tipped a hat he wasn't wearing. "Well, they've done it," he said again.

"Done what?" Hiram asked.

"They killed that cat. Trevis Wilcox and his boy shot him up in Moss Canyon and just now dragged him down. They're down in the village at the grocery-store parking lot. I thought you ought to see it."

"Why?"

"Christ, man, you're the vet around here. Not that you can help the beast now, but take a look at it and tell us if you think it's the right cat."

"The right cat? I never saw it."

Lewis Fife bit his lip and said slowly, "Well, the Newton kid said the cat he saw was a lot bigger and, you know, when you're scared everything looks bigger, but still."

"Okay, I'll come down." Hiram turned to Carolyn. "Do you want to come with me?"

"I don't need to see a dead lion. I don't think you need to see it either."

"Probably not, but I'm going anyway." Hiram looked at Carolyn's face. She disapproved, but he could see that she was not up to an argument.

"Please don't get all upset."

"I won't."

"I'll take care of him," Lewis Fife said.

Hiram and his father searched all day, went home, and then returned to the woods the following morning. Hiram watched his father's face as they rode, his chin and cheeks darkened by a thick stubble. He didn't much like his father, not because he was a bad man, not because he was mean, but because he never seemed to want more for himself, never opened books, and seemed afraid when Hiram did.

"So when we find him, Hiram, I'm going to let you have him," his father said.

"I don't want him, Dad." Hiram sucked in a deep breath. "You know, Dad, there's probably not ten wolves left in these parts. We shouldn't be killing them."

"You're gonna shoot him, all right. It'll be kind of a rite of passage for you."

Hiram didn't say anything, but a chill ran through him and he felt like crying.

From up high they could look down to the beaver pond. There were no animals around and Hiram got a bad feeling that the wolf was near. They rode down the slope slowly. Hiram's father carefully pulled his rifle from its scabbard.

And there it was. The wolf was trotting along the near side of the pond, moving upstream. His coat was dark gray and he was carrying his bushy tail high. It was a big wolf. Hiram guessed that the animal weighed over a hundred pounds. It was beautiful, moving effortlessly. He loved the wolf. And when he looked at the smile on his father's face

155

he was filled with hate. He was embarrassed by the hatred, afraid of it, sickened by it, feeling lost because of it.

"Come on, boy," Hiram's father said.

Hiram followed reluctantly. They rode down across the meadow and past the pond and then circled wide away from the creek and back to it. The wolf was standing in a thicket, just thirty yards away. Hiram could see his eyes, the rounded tops of his ears.

"He's all yours, boy," Hiram's father said.

"I can't do it," Hiram said.

"Shoot him," the man commanded. "Shoot him or you ain't no son of mine."

Hiram looked at his father's unyielding eyes.

"Shoot him."

Hiram raised the Weatherby and lined up a shot. The wolf didn't move; his eyes were as unyielding as his father's. He squeezed off the round and watched as the startled animal had only enough time to change the expression in his eyes. The wolf looked at Hiram and asked why, then fell over dead as the bullet caught him in the chest with a dull thump. A shockingly small amount of red showed through the fur.

Hiram turned to his still-smiling father and said, "I hate you."

"Fine shooting."

"You didn't hear me," Hiram said. "I hate you." He stared at his father until the man looked away. Hiram turned his horse and stepped off in the direction of the pond.

"You had to do it, Hiram. That wolf was threatening our welfare, your family," the man called after. Then, more to himself, he said, "He was killing our stock. He had to be done away with."

Hiram rode home alone, feeling scared of what his father would do when he arrived, feeling scared by what the lost spirit of the wolf was going to do to him. Tears began to slide down his face and he wished that his father could see them.

As he rode down the steep ridge above his family's home Hiram saw them in the pasture. Six dogs were chasing a small ewe, sliding on the wet grass as she made her sharp turns. Hiram was filled with such anger that he couldn't breathe, his hands mindlessly raised the rifle, and he found himself drawing a bead on one dog and then another. He fired and missed badly, but the dogs went running away. He looked up the ridge and saw his father staring down at the dogs, staring down at him. Hiram gave his horse a kick and trotted home.

He didn't speak to his mother as he stormed into the house and he felt bad because he could tell he was frightening his younger sister, sitting there at the bottom of the stairs, stroking the border collie. He marched up to his room and slammed the door. He paced from the window to the door, his hands closing and opening, closing and opening, and all he could see was the face of the wolf, indifferent and unsuspecting, the amber eyes boring into him. He wanted to scream. He heard his father's horse outside and he looked through the window to see him tying up at the post.

"I hate you!" Hiram shouted, but his father didn't look up. "I told you it was dogs! I told you!" Still his father did not raise his eyes to the second floor, but walked onto the porch and into the house.

Hiram could hear his mother asking what had happened as he threw open his bedroom door and stepped to the top of the stairs. "*He's* what happened!" Hiram said. "He made me shoot the wolf."

"That's enough, Hiram," his father said.

"No, it's not enough. You made me kill that beautiful animal because you're too stupid to listen to anybody."

Hiram's father started toward him, up the stairs. It might have been the perspective, but Hiram realized that he was larger than his father. He looked down at the man and moved to meet him on the stairs.

"Hiram," his mother complained.

His sister was crying and that was the only sound which seemed to filter through his rage.

"I said 'enough,'" his father said.

"Bastard."

Hiram saw the rage in his father's eyes and ducked his swinging fist, heard his mother's scream. Hiram grabbed the man and felt how weak he was. He now understood that his father had been profoundly affected by the death of the animal, and felt his father's chest heaving with sobs. Hiram fell to the floor holding his father, both crying, neither letting go.

It was true that Lewis Fife didn't look comfortable seated in the driver's seat of an automobile. His stomach pressed against the steering wheel, which he held with both of his fat paws, the seat belt idle beside him since it would not accommodate his girth. "Been driving for thirty-five years and not one accident," Lewis Fife would say, taking a steep curve on two wheels. Hiram sat beside him in the monstrous mid-seventies Lincoln Town Car, squeezing his nails into the armrest, believing, as did everyone else, that Lewis Fife was long overdue for a vehicular mishap. But that night the fat man didn't take any curves on two wheels, didn't drive well above the limit, didn't crowd the center line, didn't fumble with a bag of chips set on his shelf of a stomach. Lewis drove steady and slow from Hiram's house all the way to the village with his eyes stapled to the highway; the silence about him suggested reverence. Hiram was taken over by a similar quiet mood. All he could imagine was the large, majestic, dead face of the lion.

Lewis Fife pulled into the parking lot of the grocery store and parked in a space well away from a large huddle of people. They were standing around the bed of a black dually pickup with yellow running lights.

Lewis Fife pointed but didn't say anything.

Hiram grabbed the handle, opened the door, and got out. He walked toward the truck, feeling the muscles in his stomach shaking as if he were freezing cold. Beyond the crowd and the truck was the market, all lit up; people inside were pushing carts and standing in the checkout lines. He looked at the people inside, trying to distract himself, trying to tell himself that there was other business in the world. He recalled the look on Carolyn's face as he left the house and repeated to himself that he wouldn't cause a scene.

Hiram heard someone say, "Hey, it's Doc Finch." And the crowd of men peeled away from the truck and watched him. He got to the bed of the big pickup and there it was. Nothing could have prepared him for the face of the animal. He was large, his head about the size of a big boxer dog's, and the front legs were crossed in a comfortable-looking position as he lay on his side. But the face. The mouth was open, showing pink against white teeth, and the tongue hung crazily out along the metal of the truck. The ochre eyes were open and hollow and cold and held a startled expression. Hiram looked up at the faces of the surrounding men, one at a time until he saw Wilcox and his son. The two were not quite smiling.

"We got him, Doc," Wilcox said.

Hiram swallowed. "Yep, I guess you did." Hiram touched the fur of the lion's neck and stroked it.

"Big one, ain't he, Doc?" someone said.

Hiram felt Lewis Fife standing beside him. He walked away from him, circled around the open tailgate of the truck, and studied the cat. "He's a big one, all right. I hope he's the right one."

"He's the right one," Wilcox said.

"Got him in Moss Canyon," the Wilcox son said. "I shot him," proudly, a little too loudly.

Hiram looked up, caught the boy's eyes, and saw the fear in them.

The silence was then broken by a scream and the breaking of glass. Hiram turned with the others to see Marjorie Stoval a few yards away, with dropped sacks and broken bottles at her feet, looking at the lion. She screamed again and then sank to her knees, crying. Hiram went to her, as did the Wilcox boy. Hiram supported her while the boy gathered her groceries. They helped her away from the pickup and to the line of stacked wire carts in front of the store.

Hiram talked to her. "Mrs. Stoval, are you all right? Mrs. Stoval?"

The Wilcox kid backed away and rejoined his father. Hiram stood with the woman and watched the crowd disperse, watched the black dually pickup drive off down the street.

"I'm sorry you had to see that," Hiram said.

Lewis Fife came over. "Is she okay?" he asked Hiram.

Hiram shrugged.

"I'm sorry," Marjorie said, trying to stand up straight, but keeping a hand on the cart. "I've never seen anything like that."

"I know. Where's your car?" Hiram asked. Marjorie pointed across the lot toward a small station wagon. "Listen, I'm going to drive you home."

"I'll follow you," Lewis Fife said.

The headlights of the Lincoln faded and grew large, but stayed in sight the whole way. Hiram had failed to adjust the driver's seat of Marjorie Stoval's wagon and so he was crammed in behind the wheel; his knee raked his elbow every time he shifted. Marjorie was no longer crying, but sat stone-faced, staring ahead through the windshield.

"Are you okay?" Hiram asked.

"I'm so embarrassed," the woman said.

"Why should you be embarrassed? I think your reaction was the only appropriate one out there. I told them not to, but they did it. They say they did it to protect their stock. They say they did it to protect their families. But none of that is true. They did it because they're small men." Hiram felt how tightly he was holding the steering wheel in his hands, and when he glanced into the mirror, he noticed that Lewis Fife's headlights were white dots well off in the distance. He eased his foot off the accelerator and tried to relax.

"You're really upset, aren't you?" Marjorie said.

Hiram didn't answer, but did look at her.

"That was a beautiful animal," she said.

"Yes, it was."

"I saw a lion near my place once." Marjorie rolled her window partway down. "He was on the ridge about three hundred yards from my house. I couldn't believe it. It was about nine in the morning and I had just finished my tea and there he was. Or she. I don't know. I got my boots on as fast as I could and went hiking up there, but it was gone. I can still see the white tip of its tail." She closed her eyes.

Hiram looked over at her face, the curve of her nose, then down at her hands, large for a woman of her size, but they fit her. "They're magnificent creatures, all right. *Felis concolor.*"

"I'm sorry you're having to do this, drive me home, I mean."

"It's no trouble." Hiram glanced behind him. "Besides, Lewis is here to drive me home." He felt a cramp start in his leg and tried to stretch it out.

"You're kind of wedged in there."

"Yes, ma'am."

Marjorie laughed.

"I like you, Dr. Finch," she said.

Hiram nodded and smiled at her.

"I'm sorry I unloaded my baggage on you earlier." Marjorie's voice didn't sound frail anymore. "I mean, about what's-his-name."

"Eagle Nest, eh?"

"In a trailer." She shook her head. "Did I mention that she's twenty-three? I saw her. Dwight and I were shopping and we ran into her. She saw him and said hello and then she saw me and they pretended not to know each other. That's how I found out." She sneezed out a laugh.

"That sounds awful."

"Have you ever had an affair?"

"No."

"Ever thought about it?"

"No. I guess I'm pretty boring, huh?"

"I wouldn't say that," Marjorie said. "I wouldn't say that at all. In fact, I'd say you are anything but boring."

"Why, thank you kindly, ma'am."

Hiram turned off the road into Marjorie Stoval's yard and killed the engine. They were out of the car when Lewis Fife came to a complete stop. The fat man waited in his car while Hiram helped Marjorie with her groceries. He held the ruptured sacks and stood next to her on the porch while she looked for her keys. Once inside he put the groceries on the table in the kitchen.

"Well, I guess I'll see you around," Hiram said.

"I guess."

"Good night, Mrs. Stoval."

"Marjorie."

"Hiram." He smiled at her. "Good night."

Lewis Fife was more relaxed during the drive home than he had been during the ride to see the lion. He drove faster, his fat fingers holding the bottom of the steering wheel lightly.

"Seems like a nice woman," Lewis Fife said.

Hiram agreed.

"I never met her before tonight."

Hiram glanced out the window at the river as they passed it. "I've been out to treat her animals a few times. I was out at her place treating her horse just today."

"She live there by herself?"

"Yes, I believe so."

"Not married?"

Hiram shrugged. He didn't want to seem removed, but neither did he want to broadcast the woman's life story all over the county. "I think there's a Mr. Stoval, but I've never seen him."

"Funny," Lewis Fife said, "the things we assume."

Hiram looked back out his window and his thoughts turned to the lion. "I wanted to scream just like she did," he said. "I just don't get people. Did you see the look on the Wilcox boy's face?" He glanced over at the silent Lewis Fife. "He hurt that boy."

"Takes all kinds."

At home, Hiram found Carolyn already in bed and sound asleep. He didn't pause for the cup of tea he wanted, just undressed and slid into bed next to her. He felt the cool sheets against his back and stared up at the ceiling. The vapor lamp over the door of the barn always threw just a little light through the window. He listened to his wife's breathing and closed his eyes. *The world was thirty inches high and full of scents, the pads of his paws struck the ground fully, completely, feeling it thoroughly, absolutely, pushing it away beneath his body with each stride and he was floating, the muscles of his haunches and shoulders replete with eager power, power resting, power tightly wound, his nerves on fire, his eyes pressed to the edge of capacity and all of it, all of it set to the quiet his presence created in the woods, the quiet and his subdued, continuous, vibrating breathing. He understood that he was in danger, that he fell centered in the crosshairs of someone's sad and human weapon, but he could not pause to be apprehensive, could not pause to locate the enemy, but instead walked through the woods that were his, the quiet of his making, looking for life where life always was, walking on the floor that had always been his, waiting for the report to split the air. Now he was Hiram Finch and he was standing in Marjorie Stoval's kitchen, at least he believed it was Marjorie Stoval's kitchen, it being oddly made of wood with the bark still on it, and Marjorie was standing in front of him, her blouse open and her breasts exposed and he was attending to her nipples, large nipples, the kind he had never found appealing, but here they were and he wondered why he was in her kitchen and she was pushing her finger toward him, toward his chest that he realized was uncovered, to his sternum. Her finger landed lightly and he could feel his heart rattling in its cave, vibrating and filling his torso with that low, continuous purring and her finger dragged its nail down along the line that separated his left from his right. . . .* Hiram awoke with a start and saw the light from the vapor lamp still on the ceiling and heard his wife breathing beside him. He pushed the top sheet off his body and tried to let the air through the window cool him. He was afraid and lonely and hungry, terribly hungry. He rolled onto his side and faced his wife's back. He put his hand on her hair.

I GOT A GUY ONCE

Danny Gunnerson's mailbox had a serious look, like it could handle any kind of news. Someone had even painted it black, for good measure. I glanced inside to make sure the mail hadn't come, then sat down on the bumper of a blue jeep parked just off the main road. The sun was pushing through for the usual early-afternoon break in the overcast, and I'd started to sweat in my flannel shirt.

Danny owed me what was, in those days, a lot of money—about three thousand dollars. He probably owed others, which accounted for his telling everyone he was going bankrupt long before it happened. At first Danny had told me he wasn't getting checks, period. They just weren't hitting his mailbox. "The mill has quit paying," he kept telling us. "They're just stacking logs in the yard. If Japan doesn't fork over, nobody gets paid." I tried, but couldn't figure it. I knew the same company was paying boys in other outfits every two weeks.

He'd been stringing us along like a clothesline to China, and the poor prospects of timber cutting meant he could get away with it. Meanwhile, when I'd missed child-support payments, my ex-wife had turned collection over to the state. I'd moved a renter into my house as a stopgap for some kind of steady income. The state had threatened to confiscate my pickup, plus my land and everything on it, if I didn't pay up. The pickup they could have. I had even put a sign on it to warn people of its value: NOT A PIECE OF JUNK. GENUINE ARTIFACT OF SPOTTED OWL ERA. I thought tourists would appreciate the local color, since tourists were what we had of light industry these days.

But there had to be an end to Danny's stringing us along. So I worked out which day the check should be delivered to his place, then drove there to sit, big as a jaybird, near his mailbox.

Gunnerson had one of those stump ranches halfway up Lost Mountain. A wooden boat had dead-ended practically on his doorstep. Marooned near a trailer house was a lime-green sofa, minus its cushions. Half a dozen fat white geese were pulling tufts of sick-looking yellow grass between rusted vehicles and appliances.

It was peaceful to lean against the jeep with the sun hazing through, and I got to thinking about the mail carrier who'd be coming along anytime now. I knew Joe Cooper had this route, because my Aunt Trina lived up the road, and she was always telling me things Joe told her. He was an awful gossip and lady's man. I'd known Joe when he'd been a logger, back when, as they say, the getting was good—long before work in the woods got scarce, with government lands slammed shut to logging. Private timber had been coming down so fast lately that deer were sleeping on our front porches, and a cougar had snapped up a Pomeranian from a backyard near Morse Creek.

Joe hadn't quit logging because of any special eye to the future. Short and simple, he'd developed an honest bad back, like a lot of middle-aged loggers. Then he'd started having some near misses—snags crashing down at his elbow, saws jamming in the butts of trees—things that happen one time or another to anyone who stays long enough with the timber. But Joe read the writing on the wall, while the rest of us just kept getting up with the dawn, hoping for the next stand of timber to cut, even if it turned out to be smack against a playground full of kids.

"How you doing, Billy?" Joe called to me as he pulled up in front of Danny's mailbox. He leaned out the window of his snub-nosed jeep, opened the black mailbox, and, like he was sliding some awful dish into an oven, pushed Gunnerson's mail inside.

"I'm fit as a fiddle in a hailstorm," I said, and went over to Joe.

We shot the breeze and Joe allowed as how he could get me on with the postal service any time I wanted to pack it in with logging. "Your job's too dangerous," I said. "You think I don't read about those wacko postal workers who blitz their co-workers and innocent P.O.-box owners to bejesus with AK-forty-sevens? And what about mail bombs? Hazardous duty, I'd say."

"That's what a regular paycheck will do for you," Joe said. "Fearless, I'm simply fearless." But he grinned in a way that said he missed the old sawdust edge a little. He knew I'd been a gyppo logger for over thirty years and regular paychecks are just a dirty rumor to a gyppo.

"There's nothing I like better than to be in timber," I said. "I'm going to last it out until my tailbone drags the ground like a praying mantis." We had a good laugh on that one. The way he enjoyed my stubbornness let me know he envied me for staying with what I loved. He understood how, with hardly a heartbeat between, a logger can love trees and love to cut them, too.

Once Joe was out of sight, I stepped to the mailbox and reached in. I knew Gunnerson or someone must be home, because wood smoke was sifting from the chimney, one of those slow green-wood fires people in these parts light in the spring to shove back the damp. His yellow pickup, a real beater, was parked in the turnaround. It occurred to me Danny might even be watching through the window, so I tried to be quick. I shuffled the mail like it was a stacked deck and I was hunting the fifth ace. It was there, too. I brought the envelope with the return address from *"Jansik, Inc."* to the top.

This company had been buying logs as fast as we could lay down trees, then selling them to Japan. One of the long-shoremen I knew told me the trees were being used in Japan to make forms for pouring concrete in high-rises. Then, he said, the wood was tossed. I hated to think of such good wood scummed with concrete and lost to a scrap heap. It hurt me, hearing about waste I couldn't stop.

I let the Jansik envelope ride the pile—mainly bills, along with a tools catalog and some coupon packets. Then I knocked the mud off my calks on the bumper of the jeep and headed for Gunnerson's house. I braved it right through the middle of the geese, hissing when they hissed at me. I must have been convincing because they reared their heads back on their slick cobra-sized necks, then wad-dled to the side of the house. On the porch there was a kid's trike beside a refrigerator with the door ajar. Pulpy apples and limp celery stalks were sinking through the racks. I felt for Gunnerson. The dead food in his recently disabled re-frigerator reminded me he had a family to support, same as me. But he was getting his checks. It was an important dif-ference, and why I was standing on his porch with his mail in my hands.

I gave the front door a good hard-knuckle rap and tried to look in through the frosted glass. Suddenly I was nose to nose with Danny. Before he could say a thing, I handed him the mail, check envelope on top.

"What do you know about that!" I said. "Jansik paid today."

Danny looked like he was anywhere but there holding his mail. I'd worked for him many a time before this. He was a personable-enough guy. Could talk you into anything in the way of timber cutting, slash clearing, or snagging a unit, once a cut was finished. I had climbed ridges a mountain goat would have balked at, in order to cut timber for Danny Gunnerson. When the pressure was on to get logs out before closures of one sort and another, I had even cut in windstorms, one of the dumbest things an experienced faller can do. So I'm saying I had put myself out for this guy, and I wasn't ashamed to be standing there on his porch, asking for pay I deserved.

"Probably more excuses," Danny said, glancing at the envelope he'd been expecting all along. "Come in, Billy, come in," he said, and stepped back so I could see into the rooms. The place was a shambles and his wife was still in her robe, so I stayed on the porch. Danny left the door ajar while he went over to a little piled-up table in one corner that served as a desk and brought back what I hoped was a checkbook. He took the Jansik envelope and tore it open. He examined the check and groaned. "I can't believe these jackasses, shorting me like this," he said. "I can let you have three hundred," he told me when he looked up. "That's the best I can do." He made it seem a stretch. "Surely they'll pay the lot in a couple of weeks."

"Surely," I said. He found a pen on the TV and made out a check, leaning over a bronzed clock with its exhausted Indian rider. Then he folded the check in half and handed it to me like it was some kind of secret. It hit me that this was exactly what he intended. I wasn't to let on to the others at the job that I'd gotten paid even a fraction of what I was owed.

"Jake and Paul will be glad to hear the payload came in," I said, and unfolded the check to make sure I wouldn't get down the road to find he hadn't signed it. I looked up as his expression fell, then stuck the check in my shirt pocket and stepped off the porch toward my pickup.

Before the day was out, I made sure my partners got around to Danny's for their shares. In no time, I was able to have my phone turned on and to buy lumber for the out-house I was hammering together back of what I called my hovel. Fifteen years earlier, I'd built an A-frame on my acreage, complete with a beautiful stone fireplace that a logger-turned-stonemason had run twenty-six feet to the pitch of my roof. It was a monument, that fireplace. I'd packed the stones off a mountaintop myself, a few at a time in my saddlebags. Heather stone it's called, because it's found on ridges above the timberline in patches of heather.

Now another guy, a renter, a man who'd never set eyes on heather stone atop a ridge, was warming his toes at my fireplace. His kids, from various marriages and byways of desire, were scraping crayons down my walls, and his cur-rent girlfriend was burning Spam in my skillet. But what could I say? Hey, he paid his rent.

A month back I'd made this retreat to the hovel, which

I'd used as a bunkhouse during elk-hunting season. It had come in handy of late as a fall-back position when I'd had to rent my house. Having been run out of house and home, needless to say, it did not sit well when, two weeks after my mailbox visit, Danny came to us hangdog and confessed he was now truly and irreversibly bankrupt. He threw himself on our mercy. He said if we could just cut this one last section, he could maybe sell the logs for lumber to a guy he knew, then put his machinery up for sale. He promised to split the take between us and his other creditors. We knew it was one more promise he was unlikely to keep.

That very day we gathered our gear, took one last look at our spar tree, which was as good as they come—straight and well-rooted—and which we hated to leave, maybe for its resemblance to our own stripped-down lives. It was next to abandoning a brother, to walk off from that spar. But we took our saws, wedges, and falling axes and we walked out of there.

Imagine our surprise three days later when Joe Cooper stopped in at the coffee shop to tell us Danny was still in business, floating home-free on a gang of greenhorns. Naturally the new gang had been promised big pay. The truth would only hit them a couple of weeks later.

I didn't say anything to Joe when he told us this. But I had an image at the back of my mind of that great fir spar bouncing up as it fell, then rebounding several times before it settled in its lay. If the spar goes, that's it. There'd be a shutdown and a good while before another could be rigged and put into use. The thought did not let me rest. It occurred to me I would even be doing this virgin crew a favor, saving them from putting in so much as another day's work for which they would certainly never see pay.

In over thirty years of falling I had cut trees in all conditions and weather, including snow up to my nostrils, but I had never cut a tree at night. Luckily there was a bloated moon above the ridge. I was amazingly calm and not the least bit at odds with Danny as I hefted my chain saw from the pickup. I felt that all the worn-out, misused loggers, past and present, were somehow with me. Not that this would truly put right the situation between piecemeal thieves like Danny and honest, hardworking folk like Jake, Paul, and myself. The damage was too extensive and ongoing to kid myself about that. But at least this was some show of spirit.

In my twenties I'd logged with a Swede who had said, "Better to be a tiger for one day, than a sheep for a thousand." It seemed, at the time, a fairly dangerous idea. Some twenty-five years had passed. I had been a sheep a long time, had gotten comfortable in my woolly ways. But the Swede's words came back to me, there on that mountainside.

In the moonlight the spar looked silver. The block, which is used like a pulley to run cable out from it to yard in each log, was dangling at the tree's stripped crown. Guy wires were stretched to stumps. Before I could bring the block down, I would have to drop these cables. They were fastened to the stumps with railroad spikes, and I used a crowbar to pry the spikes loose. Then I cranked my saw into the tree itself.

That sound of a chain saw in moonlight—I hadn't been ready for that. It made such a raw snarl that I drew the saw blade out of the cut and throttled back. Then silence dropped over me—the velvety, deep quiet of clearcut, and above that, of trees still growing, untouched high on the ridge. It was a fresh, unwearied silence that probably belongs to the instant before the world was born. The moon seemed to look down at me and to make a great show of itself in all the blue-blackness of sky around it. I felt watched as I cranked the saw again and stepped to the spar.

I set a cut into the base, two feet from the ground. When a pull of air hit the saw, I yanked it out, just as the tree began to hinge from the stump and break into its fall. The spar gave way in slow motion. Its falling seemed so outside time that I was glad to see it finally reach the ground. On impact there was a brittle sound of machinery and I could make out the yarder crushed as easily as a beer can under the trunk.

Just as the spar rebounded I glimpsed something live making a run from the clearing. It was the size of a large dog. A cougar, I guessed, probably displaced by the recent havoc we'd wreaked on that hillside. "It's all over, here," I shouted, my voice coming back to me with too much importance. "Don't you worry," I called into the night. I was speaking to the cougar, but also to the trees, and to the stare-down moon that was shining over what I had just done.

After the spar settled, I went over and ran my hand the length of it, right up to the block, past the stove-in yarder, its snapped wires gone slack. The tree still had plenty of quiver, and I felt sorry all over again to put to waste such a perfectly good spar. At the same time a giddy lightness came over me. I felt like a man with cougar in his veins. I could have clawed my way up a hemlock or skimmed five miles at a bound. It was energy I couldn't account for. Sheep energy, built up for years, working on and off for Danny Gunnerson and the like.

Standing there in the moonlight, next to kinked iron and that downed spar, I felt that, at least for those moments, there was something peaceful in having called a line on what you were willing to put up with. Pride is an awful engine, mind you. I had been raised to keep a clear heart, not to do wrong to anyone, and if anyone asked me today, I would stand by that view of life. I would not bother to argue for rightness in what I'd just done, and done out of the usual misbegotten notions that add ruin to ruin in the world. No, this night's work was somewhere out there with cougars and bobcats, with instincts we pledge to mostly overcome. But I figured, right or wrong, that for all the daylight I'd given up to Danny Gunnerson in good faith, I had one such night coming. My mind seemed eerily far-reaching, like that moon-washed night. If an army of Danny Gunnersons were to line up in my future, I hoped maybe I'd walk away with a little more backbone for having taken that spar down, wrongheaded as it was.

The moon was sinking fast by the time I'd finished dropping the block and dragged it a hundred yards into the brush. I piled limbs and salal over it, then went back to the clearing for my saw. The spar was white as a tusk, right where I'd left it, resting on the yarder. I looked toward the edge of the clearing and thought I caught a glimmer of the cranked-up, mad-to-the-core night eyes of a cougar.

I let a day pass, but I couldn't keep away from that clearing. At daybreak on the second day I found myself near the work site with my hounds. Danny's new men had already sawed the spar for stove wood. There were fresh jets of sawdust in the dirt where they'd cut it to length. Danny was rummaging the carcass of the yarder when he saw me. "Hey, Billy," he shouted, "some son of a bitch took out my spar and my yarder." He had the brow of an angel when he said it, and it was a wonder to me that a man like Danny could carry himself so pure and so wronged. But just that quick, I saw myself—not so different from him as I had been.

My hounds were crooning, a sign the trail had suddenly gone live, and I knew they'd be high notes over the ridge in a matter of minutes, so I waved at Danny like the man of leisure I'd suddenly become, thanks to him. I put my eyes to the ground for track. I admit it did my heart good to see I'd given him pause, made him take stock of a shift in his stature in the universe. Maybe what I'd done was the start of a true downward spiral for Danny's life. All I know is, he really did go bankrupt after that.

One day five years later I was driving to Discovery Bay to shoe a horse for Joe Cooper, when I saw a man walking at the side of the road. It was pouring rain and he was thumbing without looking as he walked.

I pulled over, thinking it could be me anytime now, since I was odd-jobbing it to hold things together these days, one step ahead of the devil. The guy opened the truck door, tossed his lunch bucket onto the seat, and climbed in. When he turned his head, I saw it was Danny. He'd aged considerably, to the point it made me wonder if I looked as bad. There'd been a twinkle in his eyes in our logging days, and he'd had charm that could cause a man to put aside his better judgment.

"Billy!" he said, like I was someone he'd been missing, and he put out his hand. We caught hold of each other's palms and gave a squeeze. Rain was pelting the windshield. I could smell his clothes, wet and acrid in a mix of wood smoke and denim.

I was driving the same amazing piece of junk as when I'd worked for him, and we remarked on the sturdy nature of junk, that it should be given more credit on the world's balance sheet. "I'm not much better than a piece of junk myself," Danny said, and smiled. I was glad to hear something in his voice that meant this wasn't such a calamity for him to admit. At the same time, I saw that whatever he'd been traveling on earlier had left him. He could no longer strike deals, borrow money at banks, or convince a crew their paychecks were just around the corner.

"I'm splitting shakes in Chimacum," he told me. I looked down at one of his hands, resting palm-up near the lunch bucket, and I saw it was torn all to hell. We didn't talk for a stretch while I chanced it around a string of trailer houses leaving the west-end campgrounds in the downpour.

"I got me an indoor toilet again," I volunteered, as if to let him know I'd improved on where I'd been in our final days, when he'd joked that he'd advance me one crescent moon for my outhouse door.

What does one piece of junk say to another piece of junk anyway, going down the road? We talked a little more damage. One of his kids had turned wild as rhubarb in August, he said, and his wife's ex-husband had recently flipped his lid, rushed into their house one morning, yanked the phone off the wall, then lunged out again, using it as a walkie-talkie to God.

"I wish I had connections like that," Danny said, and

laughed in something akin to his old self. I told him how my drunken renter had run over and killed my favorite hound. I even exaggerated the state of my finances, telling him I was down to washing cars at the Jack-Pot, trying to steal customers from the cheerleaders on Sundays.

It was raining when I came to my turnoff. I pulled over to let him out. He stepped onto the roadside, then reached back into the cab and offered me his beaten-up hand again. I leaned across the seat and took it, then let it go. I looked down and waited as he slammed the truck door. For a few moments I idled in the truck and watched him start off down the road without looking back.

The amazing thing was that there was still a lot left to Danny, even with his life savvy and charm out of the way. It occurred to me that if revenge is sweet, it's because it is also more than a little sad, sad and a weight to carry. And more often than not, we mistake sadness for sweetness.

When I glanced in my side-view, Danny was swinging his black lunch bucket and holding out his thumb. Cars were passing him up, one after the other. I considered turning around and driving him to Chimacum myself, just to save having to think of him cast out that way, a man without so much as a piece of junk to drive down the road.

But the past is a sure bullet with no mission but forward. I could feel it zinging straight through the stray, half-smart thoughts I wanted to have about my life or the fate of Danny Gunnerson. So I just kept herding my piece of junk down the road, to shoe a horse for Joe Cooper, a horse not unlike Joe, with more than a few bad rumors attached to it. Joe's ten-year-old granddaughter had named the horse Renegade, a name that gave me pause, thinking how even a kid knows, without being told, that wildness ought to be honored, ought to be called to. Like a horse named Renegade, that I was about to humiliate by pounding nails into its hooves to hold on rims of steel.

LORRIE MOORE

FOUR CALLING BIRDS, THREE FRENCH HENS

When the cat died on Veterans Day, his ashes then packed into a cheesy pink-posied tin and placed high upon the mantel, the house seemed lonely and Aileen began to drink. She had lost all her ties to the animal world. She existed now in a solely man-made place: The couch was furless, the carpet dry and unmauled, the kitchen corner where the food dish had been no longer scabby with Mackerel Platter and hazardous for walking.

Oh, Bert!

He had been a beautiful cat.

Her friends interpreted the duration and intensity of her sorrow as a sign of displaced mourning: her grief was for something larger, more appropriate—it was the impending death of her parents; it was the son she and Jack had never had (though wasn't three-year-old Sofie cute as a zipper?);

it was this whole Bosnia, Cambodia, Somalia, Dinkins, Giuliani, NAFTA thing.

No, really, it was just Bert, Aileen insisted. It was just her sweet, handsome cat, her buddy of ten years. She had been with him longer than she had with either Jack or Sofie or half her friends, and he was such a smart, funny guy—big and loyal and verbal as a dog.

"What do you mean, *verbal as a dog*?" Jack scowled.

"I swear it," she said.

"Get a grip," said Jack, eyeing her glass of blended malt. Puccini's "Humming Chorus," the Brahms "Alto Rhapsody," Samuel Barber's "Adagio for Strings" all murmured in succession from the stereo. He flicked it off. "You've got a daughter. There are holidays ahead. That damn cat wouldn't have shed one tear over you."

"I really don't think that's true," she said a little wildly, perhaps with too much fire and malt in her voice. She now spoke that way sometimes, insisted on things, ventured out on a limb, lived dangerously. She had already— carefully, obediently—stepped through all the stages of bereavement: anger, denial, bargaining, Häagen-Dazs, rage. Anger to rage—who said she wasn't making progress? She made a fist but hid it. She got headaches, mostly prickly ones, but sometimes the zigzag of a migraine made its way into her skull and sat like a cheap, crazy tie in her eye.

"I'm sorry," said Jack. "Maybe he would have.

Fundraisers. Cards and letters. Who can say? You two were close, I know."

She ignored him. "Here," she said, pointing at her drink. "Have a little festive lift!" She sipped at the amber liquor, and it stung her chapped lips.

"Dewar's," said Jack, looking with chagrin at the bottle.

"Well," she said defensively, sitting up straight and buttoning her sweater. "I suppose you're out of sympathy with Dewar's. I suppose you're more of a *Do-ee.*"

"That's right," said Jack disgustedly. "That's right! And tomorrow I'm going to wake up and find I've been edged out by Truman!" He headed angrily up the stairs, while she listened for the final clomp of his steps and the cracking slam of the door.

Poor Jack: perhaps she had put him through too much. Just last spring, there had been her bunion situation—the limping, the crutch, and the big blue shoe. Then in September, there had been Mimi Andersen's dinner party, where Jack, the only nonsmoker, was made to go out on the porch while everyone else stayed inside and lit up. And *then*, there had been Aileen's one-woman performance of "the housework version of *Lysistrata.*" "No Sweepie, No Kissie," Jack had called it. But it had worked. Sort of. For about two weeks. There was, finally, only so much one woman on the vast and wicked stage could do.

"I'm worried about you," said Jack in bed. "I'm being earnest here. And not in the Hemingway sense, either." He screwed up his face. "You see how I'm talking? Things are wacko around here." Their bookcase headboard was so stacked with novels and sad memoirs, it now resembled a library carrel more than a conjugal bed.

"You're fine. I'm fine. Everybody's fine," said Aileen. She tried to find his hand under the covers, then just gave up.

"You're someplace else," he said. "Where are you?"

The birds had become emboldened, slowly reclaiming the yard, filling up the branches, cheeping hungrily in the mornings from the sills and eaves. "What is that *shriek-ing*?" Aileen asked. The leaves had fallen, but now jays, ravens, and house finches darkened the trees—some of them flying south, some of them staying on, pecking the hardening ground for seeds. Squirrels moved in poking through the old apples that had dropped from the flower-ing crab. A possum made a home for himself under the porch, thumping and chewing. Raccoons had discovered Sofie's little gym set, and one morning Aileen looked out and saw two of them swinging on the swings. She'd wanted animal life? Here was animal life!

"Not this," she said. "None of this would be happening if Bert were still here." Bert had patrolled the place. Bert had kept things in line.

"Are you talking to me?" asked Jack.

"I guess not," she said.

"What?"

"I think we need to douse this place in repellent."

"You mean, like, bug spray?"

"Bug spray, Bugs Bunny," chanted Sofie. "Bug spray, Bugs Bunny."

"I don't know what I mean," said Aileen.

At her feminist film-critique group, they were still discussing *Cat Man,* a movie done entirely in flashback from the moment a man jumps off the ledge of an apartment building. Instead of being divided into acts or chapters, the movie was divided into floor numbers, in descending order. At the end of the movie, the handsome remembering man lands on his feet.

Oh, Bert!

One of the women in Aileen's group—Lila Conch—was angry at the movie. "I just hated the way anytime a woman character said anything of substance, she also happened to be half naked."

Aileen sighed. "Actually, I found those parts of the film the most true to life," she said. "Those were the parts I liked best."

The group looked at her sternly. "Aileen," said Lila, recrossing her legs. "Go to the kitchen for us, dear, and set up the brownies and tea."

"Really?" asked Aileen.

"Really," said Lila.

Thanksgiving came and went in a mechanical way. Aileen and Jack, with Sofie, went out to a restaurant and ordered different things, as if the three of them were strangers asserting their ornery tastes. Then they drove home. Only Sofie, who had ordered the child's Stuffed Squash, was somehow pleased, sitting in the back car seat and singing a Thanksgiving song she'd learned at day care. "'Oh, a turkey's not a pig, you doink / He doesn't say *oink* / He says *gobble, gobble, gobble.*'" Their last truly good holiday had been Halloween, when Bert was still alive and they had dressed him up as Jack. They'd then dressed Jack as Bert, Aileen as Sofie, and Sofie as Aileen. "Now, I'm you, Mommy," Sofie had said when Aileen had tied one of her kitchen aprons around her and pressed lipstick onto her mouth. Jack came up and rubbed his Magic Marker whiskers against Aileen, who giggled in her large pink footie pajamas. The only one who wasn't having that much fun was Bert himself, sporting one of Jack's ties, and pawing at it to get it off. When he didn't succeed, he gamely dragged the tie around for a while, trying to ignore it. Then, cross and humiliated, he waddled over to the corner near the piano and lay there, annoyed. Remembering this, a week later—when Bert was dying in an oxygen tent at the vet's, heart failing, fluid around his lungs (though his ears still pricked up when Aileen came to visit him; she wore her usual perfume so he would know her smell, and handfed him cat snacks when no one else could get him to eat)—Aileen had felt overwhelmed with sorrow and regret.

"I think you should see someone," said Jack.

"Are we talking a psychiatrist or an affair?"

"An affair, of course." Jack scowled. "An *affair*?"

"I don't know." Aileen shrugged. The whiskey she'd been drinking lately had caused her joints to swell, so that now when she lifted her shoulders, they just kind of stayed like that, stiffly, up around her ears.

Jack rubbed her upper arm, as if he either loved her or was wiping something off on her sleeve. Which could it be? "Life is a long journey across a wide country," he said. "Sometimes the weather's good. Sometimes it's bad. Sometimes it's so bad, your car goes off the road."

"Really."

"Just go talk to someone," he said. "Our health plan will cover part."

"Okay," she said. "Okay. Just—no more metaphors."

She got recommendations, made lists and appointments, conducted interviews.

"I have a death-of-a-pet situation," she said. "How long does it take for you to do those?"

"I beg your pardon?"

"How long will it take you to get me over the death of my cat, and how much do you charge for it?"

Each of the psychiatrists, in turn, with their slightly different outfits, and slightly different potted plants, looked shocked.

"Look," Aileen said. "Forget Prozac. Forget Freud's abandonment of the seduction theory. Forget Jeffrey Masson—or is it *Jackie* Mason? The only thing that's going to revolutionize *this* profession is Bidding the Job!"

"I'm afraid we don't work that way," she was told again and again—until finally, at last, she found someone who did.

"I specialize in Christmas," said the psychotherapist, a man named Sidney Poe, who wore an argyle sweater vest, a crisp bow tie, shiny black oxfords, and no socks. "Christmas specials. You feel better by Christmas, or your last session's free."

"I like the sound of that," said Aileen. It was already December first. "I like the sound of that a lot."

"Good," he said, giving her a smile that, she had to admit, looked crooked and unsound. "Now, what are we dealing with here, a cat or a dog?"

"A cat," she said.

"Whoa-boy." He wrote something down, muttered, looked dismayed.

"Can I ask you a question first?" asked Aileen.

"Certainly," he said.

"Do you offer Christmas specials because of the high suicide rates around Christmas?"

" 'The high suicide rates around Christmas,' " he repeated in an amused and condescending way. "It's a myth, the high suicide rates around Christmas. It's the *homicide* rate that's high. Holiday homicide. All that time the family suddenly gets to spend together, and then *bam,* that *eggnog.*"

She went to Sidney Poe on Thursdays—"Advent Thursdays," she called them. She sat before him with a box of designer Kleenex on her lap, recalling Bert's finer qualities and golden moments, his great sense of humor and witty high jinks. "He used to try to talk on the phone, when *I* was on the phone. And once, when I was looking for my keys, I said aloud, Where're my keys? and he came running into the room, thinking I'd said, Where's my *kitty*?"

Only once did she actually have to slap Sidney awake—lightly. Mostly, she could just clap her hands once and call his name—*Sid!*—and he would jerk upright in his psychiatrist's chair, staring wide.

"In the intensive care unit at the animal hospital," Aileen continued, "I saw a cat who'd been shot in the spine with a BB. I saw dogs recovering from jaw surgery. I saw a retriever who'd had a hip replacement come out into the lobby dragging a little cart behind him. He was so happy to see his owner. He dragged himself toward her and she knelt down and spread her arms wide to greet him. She sang out to him and cried. It was the animal version of *Porgy and Bess.*" She paused for a minute. "It made me wonder what was going on in this country. It made me think we should ask ourselves, What in hell's going on?"

"I'm afraid we're over our time," said Sidney.

The next week, she went to the mall first. She wandered in and out of the stores with their thick tinsel and treacly,

Muzak Christmas carols. Everywhere she went, there were little cat Christmas books, cat Christmas cards, cat Christmas wrapping paper. She hated these cats. They were boring, dopey, caricatured, interchangeable—not a patch on Bert.

"I had great hopes for Bert," she said later to Sidney. "They gave him all the procedures, all the medications—but the drugs knocked his kidneys out. When the doctor suggested putting him to sleep, I said, 'Isn't there anything else we can do?' and you know what the doctor said? He said, 'Yes. An autopsy.' A thousand dollars later and he says, 'Yes. An autopsy.'"

"Eeeeyew," said Sid.

"A cashectomy," said Aileen. "They gave poor Bert a cashectomy!" And here she began to cry, thinking of the sweet, dire look on Bert's face in the oxygen tent, the bandaged tube in his paw, the wet fog in his eyes. It was not an animal's way to die like that, but she had subjected him to the full medical treatment, signed him up for all that metallic and fluorescent voodoo, not knowing what else to do.

"Tell me about Sofie."

Aileen sighed. Sofie was adorable. Sofie was terrific. "She's fine. She's great." Except Sofie was getting little notes sent home with her from day care. "Today, Sofie gave the teacher the finger—except it was her index finger." Or "Today, Sofie drew a mustache on her face." Or "Today, Sofie demanded to be called Walter."

"Really."

"Our last really good holiday was Halloween. I took her trick-or-treating around the neighborhood, and she was so cute. It was only by the end of the night that she began to catch on to the whole concept of it. Most of the time, she was so excited, she'd ring the bell, and when someone came to the door, she'd thrust out her bag and say, 'Look! I've got treats for you!'"

Aileen had stood waiting, down off the porches, on the sidewalk, in her big pink footie pajamas. She'd let Sofie do the talking. "I'm my mommy and my mommy's me," Sofie explained.

"I see," said the neighbors. And then they'd call and wave from the doorway. "Hello, Aileen! How are you doing?"

"We've got to focus on Christmas here," said Sidney.

"Yes," said Aileen despairingly. "We've only got one more week."

On the Thursday before Christmas, she felt flooded with memories: the field mice, the day trips, the long naps together. "He had limited notes to communicate his needs," she said. "He had his 'food' mew, and I'd follow him to his dish. He had his 'out' mew, and I'd follow him to the door. He had his 'brush' mew, and I'd go with him to the cupboard where his brush was kept. And then he had his existential mew, where I'd follow him vaguely around the house as he wandered in and out of rooms, not knowing exactly what or why."

Sidney's eyes began to well. "I can see why you miss him," he said.

"You can?"

"Of course! But that's all I can leave you with."

"The Christmas special's up?"

"I'm afraid so," he said, standing. He reached to shake her hand. "Call me after the holiday and let me know how you feel."

"All right," she said sadly. "I will."

She went home, poured herself a drink, stood by the mantel. She picked up the pink-posied tin and shook it, afraid she might hear the muffled banging of bones, but she heard nothing. "Are you sure it's even him?" Jack asked. "With animals, they probably do mass incinerations. One scoop for cats, two for dogs."

"Please." she said. At least she had not buried Bert in the local pet cemetery, with its intricate gravestones and maudlin inscriptions—*Beloved Rexie: I'll be joining you soon.* Or, *In memory of Bluephyan, who taught me how to love.*

"I got the very last Christmas tree," said Jack. "It was leaning against the shed wall with a broken high heel and a cigarette dangling from its mouth. I thought I'd bring it home and feed it soup."

At least she had sought something more tasteful than the cemetery, sought the appropriate occasion to return him to the earth and sky, get him down off the fireplace and out of the house in a meaningful way, though she'd yet to find the right day. She had let him stay on the mantel and had mourned him deeply—it was only proper. You couldn't pretend you had lost nothing. A good cat had died—you had to begin there, not let your blood freeze over. If your heart turned away at this, it would turn away at something greater, then more and more until your heart stayed averted, immobile, your imagination redistributed away from the world and back only toward the bad maps of yourself, the sour pools of your own pulse, your own tiny, mean, and pointless wants. Stop here! Begin here! Begin with Bert!

Here's to Bert!

Early Christmas morning, she woke Sofie and dressed her warmly in her snowsuit. There was a light snow on the ground and a wind blew powdery gusts around the yard. "We're going to say good-bye to Bert," said Aileen.

"Oh, Bert!" said Sofie, and she began to cry.

"No, it'll be happy!" said Aileen, feeling the pink-posied tin in her jacket pocket. "He wants to go out. Do you re-member how he used to want to go out? How he would mee-ow at the door and then we would let him go?"

"Mee-ow, mee-ow," said Sofie.

"Right," said Aileen. "So that's what we're going to do now."

"Will he be with Santa Claus?"

"Yes! He'll be with Santa Claus!"

They stepped outside, down off the porch steps. Aileen pried open the tin: Inside, there was a small plastic bag and she tore that open. Inside was Bert: a pebbly ash like the sand and ground shells of a beach. Summer in December! What was Christmas if not a giant mixed metaphor? What was it about if not the mystery of interspecies love—God's for man! Love had sought a chasm to leap across and landed itself right here: the Holy Ghost among the barn animals, the teacher's pet sent to be adored and then to die. Aileen and Sofie each seized a fistful of Bert and ran around the yard, letting wind take the ash and scatter it. Chickadees flew from the trees. Frightened squirrels headed for the yard next door. In freeing Bert, perhaps they would become him a little: banish the interlopers, police the borders, then go back inside and play with the decorations, claw at the gift wrap, eat the big headless bird.

"Merry Christmas to Bert!" Sofie shouted. The tin was now empty.

"Yes, Merry Christmas to Bert!" said Aileen. She shoved the tin back into her pocket. Then she and Sofie raced back into the house to get warm.

Jack was in the kitchen, standing by the stove, still in his pajamas. He was pouring orange juice and heating buns.

"Daddy, Merry Christmas to Bert!" Sofie popped open the snaps of her snowsuit.

"Yes," said Jack, turning. "Merry Christmas to Bert!"

He handed Sofie some juice, then Aileen. But before she drank hers, Aileen waited for him to say something else. He cleared his throat and stepped forward. He raised his glass. His large quizzical smile said, This is a very weird family. But instead, he exclaimed, "Merry Christmas to everyone in the whole wide world!" and let it go at that.

SIMON J. ORTIZ

MEN ON THE MOON

I

Joselita brought her father, Faustin, the TV on Father's Day. She brought it over after Sunday mass, and she had her son hook up the antenna. She plugged the TV cord into the wall socket.

Faustin sat on a worn couch. He was covered with an old coat. He had worn that coat for twenty years.

It's ready. Turn it on and I'll adjust the antenna, Amarosho told his mother. The TV warmed up and then the screen flickered into dull light. It was snowing. Amarosho turned it a bit. It snowed less and then a picture formed.

Look, Naishtiya, Joselita said. She touched her father's hand and pointed at the TV.

I'll turn the antenna a bit and you tell me when the picture is clear, Amarosho said. He climbed on the roof again.

After a while the picture turned clearer. It's better! his mother shouted. There was only the tiniest bit of snow falling.

That's about the best it can get, I guess, Amarosho said. Maybe it'll clear up on the other channels. He turned the selector. It was clearer on another channel.

There were two men struggling mightily with each other. Wrestling, Amarosho said.

Do you want to watch wrestling? Two men are fighting, Nana. One of them is Apache Red. Chisheh tsah, he told his grandfather.

The old man stirred. He had been staring intently into the TV. He wondered why there was so much snow at first. Now there were two men fighting. One of them was a Chisheh—an Apache—and the other was a Mericano. There were people shouting excitedly and clapping hands within the TV.

The two men backed away from each other for a moment and then they clenched again. They wheeled mightily and suddenly one threw the other. The old man smiled. He wondered why they were fighting.

Something else showed on the TV screen. A bottle of wine was being poured. The old man liked the pouring sound and he moved his mouth and lips. Someone was selling wine.

The two fighting men came back on the TV. They struggled with each other, and after a while one of them didn't get up. And then another man came and held up the hand of the Apache, who was dancing around in a feathered headdress.

It's over, Amarosho announced. Apache Red won the fight, Nana.

The Chisheh won. Faustin stared at the other fighter, a light-haired man who looked totally exhausted and angry with himself. The old man didn't like the Apache too much. He wanted them to fight again.

After a few minutes, something else appeared on the TV.

What is that? Faustin asked. In the TV picture was an object with smoke coming from it. It was standing upright.

Men are going to the moon, Nana, Amarosho said. That's Apollo. It's going to fly three men to the moon.

That thing is going to fly to the moon?

Yes, Nana, his grandson said.

What is it called again? Faustin asked.

Apollo, a spaceship rocket, Joselita told her father.

The Apollo spaceship stood on the ground, emitting clouds of something, something that looked like smoke.

A man was talking, telling about the plans for the flight, what would happen, that it was almost time. Faustin could not understand the man very well because he didn't know many words in the language of the Mericano.

He must be talking about that thing flying in the air? he said.

Yes. It's about ready to fly away to the moon.

Faustin remembered that the evening before he had looked at the sky and seen that the moon was almost in the middle phase. He wondered if it was important that the men get to the moon.

Are those men looking for something on the moon, Nana? he asked his grandson.

They're trying to find out what's on the moon, Nana. What kind of dirt and rocks there are and to see if there's any water. Scientist men don't believe there is any life on the moon. The men are looking for knowledge, Amarosho said to Faustin.

Faustin wondered if the men had run out of places to look for knowledge on the earth. Do they know if they'll find knowledge? he asked.

They have some already. They've gone before and come back. They're going again.

Did they bring any back?

They brought back some rocks, Amarosho said.

Rocks. Faustin laughed quietly. The American scientist men went to search for knowledge on the moon and they brought back rocks. He kind of thought that perhaps Amarosho was joking with him. His grandson had gone to Indian School for a number of years, and sometimes he would tell his grandfather some strange and funny things.

The old man was suspicious. Sometimes they joked around. Rocks. You sure that's all they brought back? he said. Rocks!

That's right, Nana, only rocks and some dirt and pictures they made of what it looks like on the moon.

The TV picture was filled with the rocket spaceship close-up now. Men were sitting and standing and moving around some machinery, and the TV voice had become more urgent. The old man watched the activity in the picture intently but with a slight smile on his face.

Suddenly it became very quiet, and the TV voice was firm and commanding and curiously pleading. Ten, nine, eight, seven, six, five, four, three, two, one, liftoff. The white smoke became furious, and a muted rumble shook through the TV. The rocket was trembling and the voice was trembling.

It was really happening, the old man marveled. Somewhere inside of that cylinder with a point at its top and long slender wings were three men who were flying to the moon.

The rocket rose from the ground. There were enormous clouds of smoke and the picture shook. Even the old man became tense, and he grasped the edge of the couch. The rocket spaceship rose and rose.

There's fire coming out of the rocket, Amarosho explained. That's what makes it fly.

Fire. Faustin had wondered what made it fly. He had seen pictures of other flying machines. They had long wings, and someone had explained to him that there was machinery inside which spun metal blades that made the machines fly. He had wondered what made this thing fly. He hoped his grandson wasn't joking him.

After a while there was nothing but the sky. The rocket Apollo had disappeared. It hadn't taken very long, and the voice on the TV wasn't excited anymore. In fact, the voice was very calm and almost bored.

I have to go now, Naishtiya, Joselita told her father. I have things to do.

Me too, Amarosho said.

Wait, the old man said, wait. What shall I do with this thing? What is it you call it?

TV, his daughter said. You watch it. You turn it on and you watch it.

I mean how do you stop it? Does it stop like the radio, like the mahkina? It stops?

This way, Nana, Amarosho said and showed his grandfather. He turned a round knob on the TV and the picture went away.

He turned the knob again, and the picture flickered on again. Were you afraid this one-eye would be looking at you all the time? Amarosho laughed and gently patted the old man's shoulder.

Faustin was relieved. Joselita and her son left. Faustin watched the TV picture for a while. A lot of activity was going on, a lot of men were moving among machinery, and a couple of men were talking. And then the spaceship rocket was shown again.

The old man watched it rise and fly away again. It disappeared again. There was nothing but the sky. He turned the knob and the picture died away. He turned it on and the picture came on again. He turned it off. He went outside and to a fence a short distance from his home. When he finished peeing, he zipped up his pants and studied the sky for a while.

II

That night, he dreamed.

Flintwing Boy was watching a Skquuyuh mahkina come down a hill. The mahkina made a humming noise. It was walking. It shone in the sunlight. Flintwing Boy moved to a better position to see. The mahkina kept on moving toward him.

The Skquuyuh mahkina drew closer. Its metal legs stepped upon trees and crushed growing flowers and grass. A deer bounded away frightened. Tsushki came running to Flintwing Boy.

Anahweh, Tsushki cried, trying to catch his breath.

What is it, Anahweh? You've been running, Flintwing Boy said.

The coyote was staring at the thing, which was coming toward them. There was wild fear in his eyes.

What is that, Anahweh? What is that thing? Tsushki gasped.

It looks like a mahkina, but I've never seen one quite like

it before. It must be some kind of Skquuyuh mahkina, Anahweh, Flintwing Boy said. When he saw that Tsushki was trembling with fear, he said, Sit down, Anahweh. Rest yourself. We'll find out soon enough.

The Skquuyuh mahkina was undeterred. It walked over and through everything. It splashed through a stream of clear water. The water boiled and streaks of oil flowed downstream. It split a juniper tree in half with a terrible crash. It crushed a boulder into dust with a sound of heavy metal. Nothing stopped the Skquuyuh mahkina. It hummed.

Anahweh, Tsushki cried, what can we do?

Flintwing Boy reached into the bag hanging at his side. He took out an object. It was flint arrowhead. He took out some cornfood.

Come over here, Anahweh. Come over here. Be calm, he motioned to the frightened coyote. He touched the coyote in several places on his body with the arrowhead and put cornfood in the palm of his hand.

This way, Flintwing Boy said. He closed Tsushki's fingers over the cornfood. They stood facing east. Flintwing Boy said, We humble ourselves again. We look in your direction for guidance. We ask for your protection. We humble our poor bodies and spirits because only you are the power and the source and the knowledge. Help us, then. That is all we ask.

Flintwing Boy and Tsushki breathed on the cornfood, then took in the breath of all directions and gave the cornfood unto the ground.

Now the ground trembled with the awesome power of the Skquuyuh mahkina. Its humming vibrated against everything.

Flintwing Boy reached over his shoulder and took several arrows from his quiver. He inspected them carefully and without any rush he fit one to his bowstring.

And now, Anahweh, Flintwing Boy said, you must go and tell everyone. Describe what you have seen. The people must talk among themselves and learn what this is about, and decide what they will do. You must hurry, but you must not alarm the people. Tell them I am here to meet the Skquuyuh mahkina. Later I will give them my report.

Tsushki turned and began to run. He stopped several yards away. Hahtrudzaimeh! he called to Flintwing Boy. Like a man of courage, Anahweh, like our people.

The old man stirred in his sleep. A dog was barking. He awoke fully and got out of his bed and went outside. The moon was past the midpoint, and it would be daylight in a few hours.

III

Later, the spaceship reached the moon.

Amarosho was with his grandfather Faustin. They watched a TV replay of two men walking on the moon.

So that's the men on the moon, Faustin said.

Yes, Nana, there they are, Amarosho said.

There were two men inside of heavy clothing, and they carried heavy-looking equipment on their backs.

The TV picture showed a closeup of one of them and indeed there was a man's face inside of glass. The face moved its mouth and smiled and spoke, but the voice seemed to be separate from the face.

It must be cold, Faustin said. They have on heavy clothing.

It's supposed to be very cold and very hot on the moon. They wear special clothes and other things for protection from the cold and heat, Amarosho said.

The men on the moon were moving slowly. One of them skipped like a boy, and he floated alongside the other.

The old man wondered if they were underwater. They seem to be able to float, he said.

The information I have heard is that a man weighs less on the moon than he does on earth, Amarosho said to his grandfather. Much less, and he floats. And there is no air on the moon for them to breathe, so those boxes on their backs carry air for them to breathe.

A man weighs less on the moon, the old man thought. And there is no air on the moon except for the boxes on their backs. He looked at Amarosho, but his grandson did not seem to be joking with him.

The land on the moon looked very dry. It looked like it had not rained for a long, long time. There were no trees, no plants, no grass. Nothing but dirt and rocks, a desert.

Amarosho had told him that men on earth—scientists—

believed there was no life on the moon. Yet those men were trying to find knowledge on the moon. Faustin wondered if perhaps they had special tools with which they could find knowledge even if they believed there was no life on the moon.

The mahkina sat on the desert. It didn't make a sound. Its metal feet were planted flat on the ground. It looked somewhat awkward. Faustin searched around the mahkina, but there didn't seem to be anything except the dry land on the TV. He couldn't figure out the mahkina. He wasn't sure whether it moved and could cause harm. He didn't want to ask his grandson that question.

After a while, one of the bulky men was digging in the ground. He carried a long, thin tool with which he scooped up dirt and put it into a container. He did this for a while.

Is he going to bring the dirt back to earth too? Faustin asked.

I think he is, Nana, Amarosho said. Maybe he'll get some rocks too. Watch.

Indeed, several minutes later, the man lumbered over to a pile of rocks and gathered several handsized ones. He held them out proudly. They looked just like rocks from around anyplace. The voice on the TV seemed to be excited about the rocks.

They will study the rocks, too, for knowledge?

Yes, Nana.

What will they use the knowledge for, Nana?

They say they will use it to better mankind, Nana. I've heard that. And to learn more about the universe in which we live. Also, some of the scientists say the knowledge will be useful in finding out where everything began a long time ago and how everything was made in the beginning.

Faustin looked with a smile at his grandson. He said, You are telling me the true facts, aren't you?

Why, yes, Nana. That's what they say. I'm not just making it up, Amarosho said.

Well then, do they say why they need to know where and how everything began? Hasn't anyone ever told them?

I think other people have tried to tell them but they want to find out for themselves, and also they claim they don't know enough and need to know more and for certain, Amarosho said.

The man in the bulky suit had a small pickax in his hand. He was striking at a boulder. The breathing of the man could be heard clearly. He seemed to be working very hard and was very tired.

Faustin had once watched a work crew of Mericano drilling for water. They had brought a tall mahkina with a loud motor. The mahkina would raise a limb at its center to its very top and then drop it with a heavy and loud metal clang. The mahkina and its men sat at one spot for several days, and finally they found water.

The water had bubbled out weakly, gray-looking, and did not look drinkable at all. And then the Mericano workmen lowered the mahkina, put their equipment away, and drove away. The water stopped flowing. After a couple of days, Faustin went and checked out the place.

There was nothing there except a pile of gray dirt and an indentation in the ground. The ground was already dry, and there were dark spots of oil-soaked dirt.

Faustin decided to tell Amarosho about the dream he had had.

After the old man finished, Amarosho said, Old man, you're telling me the truth now, aren't you? You know that you've become somewhat of a liar. He was teasing his grandfather.

Yes, Nana. I have told you the truth as it occurred to me that night. Everything happened like that except I might not have recalled everything about it.

That's some story, Nana, but it's a dream.

It's a dream, but it's the truth, Faustin said.

I believe you, Nana, his grandson said.

IV

Some time after that the spacemen returned to earth. Amarosho told his grandfather they had splashed down in the ocean.

Are they alright? Faustin asked.

Yes, Amarosho said. They have devices to keep them safe.

Are they in their homes now?

No, I think they have to be someplace where they can't contaminate anything. If they brought back something from the moon that they weren't supposed to, they won't pass it on to someone else, Amarosho said to his grandfather.

What would that something be?

Something harmful, Nana.

In that dry desert land of the moon there might be something harmful, the old man said. I didn't see any strange insects or trees or even cactus. What would that harmful thing be, Nana?

Disease which might harm people on earth, Amarosho said.

You said there was the belief by the men that there is no life on the moon. Is there life after all? Faustin asked.

There might be the tiniest bit of life.

Yes, I see now, Nana. If the men find even the tiniest bit of life on the moon, then they will believe, the old man said.

Yes. Something like that.

Faustin figured it out now. The Mericano men had taken that trip in a spaceship rocket to the moon to find even the tiniest bit of life. And when they found even the tiniest bit of life, even if it was harmful, they would believe that they had found knowledge. Yes, that must be the way it was.

He remembered his dream clearly now. The old man was relieved.

When are those two men fighting again, Nana? he asked Amarosho.

What two men?

Those two men who were fighting with each other the day those Mericano spaceship men were flying to the moon.

Oh, those men. I don't know, Nana. Maybe next Sunday. You like them?

Yes. I think the next time I will be cheering for the Chisheh. He'll win again. He'll beat the Mericano again, Faustin said.

RICK DEMARINIS

WEEDS

A black helicopter flapped out of the morning sun and dumped its sweet orange mist on our land instead of the Parley farm where it was intended. It was weedkiller, something strong enough to wipe out leafy spurge, knapweed, and Canadian thistle, but it made us sick.

My father had a fatal stroke a week after that first spraying. I couldn't hold down solid food for nearly a month and went from 200 pounds to 170 in that time. Mama went to bed and slept for two days, and when she woke up she was not the same. She'd lost something of herself in that long sleep, and something that wasn't herself had replaced it.

Then it hit the animals. We didn't have much in the way of animals, but one by one they dropped. The chickens, the geese, the two old mules—Doc and Rex—and last of all, our only cow, Miss Milky, who was more or less the family pet.

Miss Milky was the only animal that didn't outright up and die. She just got sick. There was blood in her milk and her milk was thin. Her teats got so tender and brittle that she would try to mash me against the milk stall wall when I pulled at them. The white part of her eyes looked like fresh meat. Her piss was so strong that the green grass wherever she stood died off. She got so bound up that when she'd lift her tail and bend with strain, only one black apple would drop. Her breath took on a burning sulfurous stink that would make you step back.

She also went crazy. She'd stare at me like she all at once had a desperate human mind and had never seen me before. Then she'd act as if she wanted to slip a horn under my ribs and peg me to the barn. She would drop her head and charge, blowing like a randy bull, and I would have to scramble out of the way. Several times I saw her gnaw on her hooves or stand stock-still in water up to her blistered teats. Or she would walk backward all day long, mewling like a lost cat that had been dropped off in a strange place. That mewling was enough to make you want to clap a set of noise dampers on your ears. The awful sound led Mama to say this: "It's the death song of the land, mark my words."

Mama never talked like that before in her life. She'd always been a cheerful woman who could never see the bad part of anything that was at least fifty percent good. But now she was dark and careful as a gypsy. She would have spells of derangement during which she'd make noises like a wild animal, or she'd play the part of another person—the sort of person she'd normally have nothing to do with at all. At Daddy's funeral she got dressed up in an old and tattered evening gown the color of beet juice, her face painted and powdered like that of a barfly. And while the preacher told the onlookers what a fine man Daddy had been, Mamma cupped her hands under her breasts and lifted them high, as if offering to appease a dangerous stranger. Then, ducking her head, she chortled, "Loo, loo, loo," her scared eyes scanning the trees for owls.

I was twenty-eight years old and my life had come to nothing. I'd had a girl but I'd lost her through neglect and a careless attitude that had spilled over into my personal life, souring it. I had no ambition to make something worthwhile of myself and it nettled her. Toward the end she began to parrot her mother: "You need to get yourself *established, Jack,*" she would say. But I didn't want to get myself established. I was getting poorer and more aimless day by day. I supposed she believed that "getting established" would put a stop to my downhill slide but I had no desire to do whatever it took to accomplish that.

Shortly after Daddy died, the tax man came to our door with a paper in his hand. "Inheritance tax," he said, handing me the paper.

"What do you mean?" I asked.

"It's the law," he said. "Your father died, you see. And that's going to cost you some. You should have made better plans." He tapped his forehead with his finger and winked. He had a way of expressing himself that made me think he was country born and raised but wanted to seem citified. Or maybe it was the other way around.

"I don't understand this," I mumbled. I felt the weight of a world I'd so far been able to avoid. It was out there, tight-assed and squinty-eyed, and it knew to the dollar and dime what it needed to keep itself in business.

"Simple," he said. "Pay or move off. The government is the government and it can't bend a rule to accommodate the confused. It's your decision. Pay or the next step is litigation."

He smiled when he said good-bye. I closed the door against the weight of his smile, which was the weight of the world. I went to a window and watched him head back to his government green car. The window was open and I could hear him. He was singing loudly in a fine tenor voice. He raised his right hand to hush an invisible audience that had broken into uncontrolled applause. I could still hear him singing as he slipped the car into gear and idled away. He was singing "Red River Valley."

Even though the farm was all ours, paid up in full, we had to give the government $7000 for the right to stay on it. The singing tax man said we had inherited the land from my father, and the law was sharp on the subject.

I didn't know where the money was going to come from. I didn't talk it over with Mama because even in her better moments she would talk in riddles. To a simple question such as, "Should I paint the barns this year, Mama?" she might answer, "I've no eyes for glitter, nor ears for their ridicule."

One day I decided to load Miss Milky into the stock trailer and haul her into Saddle Butte where the vet, Doc Nevers, had his office. Normally, Doc Nevers would come out to your place but he'd heard about the spraying that was going on and said he wouldn't come within three miles of our property until they were done.

The Parley farm was being sprayed regularly, for they grew an awful lot of wheat and almost as much corn and they had the biggest haying operation in the county. Often the helicopters they used were upwind from us and we were sprayed too. ("Don't complain," said Big Pete Parley when I called him up about it. "Think of it this way— you're getting your place weeded for free!" When I said I might have to dynamite some stumps on the property line and that he might get a barn or two blown away for free, he just laughed like hell, as if I had told one of the funniest jokes he'd ever heard.)

There was a good windbreak between our places, a thick grove of lombardy poplars, but the orange mist, sweet as a flower garden in spring bloom, sifted through the trees and settled on our field. Soon the poplars were mottled and dying. Some branches curled in an upward twist, as if flexed in pain, and others became soft and fibrous as if the wood were trying to turn itself into sponge.

With Miss Milky in the trailer, I sat in the truck sipping on a pint of Lewis and Clark bourbon and looking out across our unplanted fields. It was late—almost too late—to plant anything. Mama, in the state she was in, hadn't even noticed.

In the low hills on the north side of the property, some ugly-looking things were growing. From the truck they looked like white pimples on the smooth brown hill. Up close they were big as melons. They were some kind of fungus and they pushed up through the ground like the bald heads of fat babies. They gave off a rotten meat stink. I would get chillbumps just looking at them and if I touched one my stomach would rise. The bulbous heads had purple streaks on them that looked like blood vessels. I half expected to one day see human eyes clear the dirt and open. Big pale eyes that would see me and carry my image down to their deepest root. I was glad they seemed to prefer the hillside and bench and not the bottom land.

Justified or not, I blamed the growth of this fungus on the poison spray, just as I blamed it for the death of my father, the loss of our animals, and the strangeness of my mother. Now the land itself was becoming strange. And I thought, what about me? How am I being rearranged by that weedkiller?

I guess I should have gotten mad, but I didn't. Maybe I *had* been changed by the spray. Where once I had been a quick-to-take-offense hothead, I was now docile and thoughtful. I could sit on a stump and think for hours, enjoying the slow and complicated intertwinings of my own thoughts. Even though I felt sure the cause of all our troubles had fallen out of the sky, I would hold arguments with myself, as if there were always two sides to every question. If I said to myself, "Big Pete Parley has poisoned my family and farm and my father is dead because of it," I would follow it up with, "But Daddy was old anyway, past seventy-five and he always had high blood pressure. Anything could have touched off his stroke, from a wasp bite to a sonic boom."

"And what about Mama?" I would ask. "Senile with grief," came the quick answer. "Furthermore, Daddy himself used poison in his time. Cyanide traps for coyotes, DDT for mosquito larvae, arsenic for rats."

My mind was always doubling back on itself in this way and it would often leave me standing motionless in a field for hours, paralyzed with indecision, sighing like a moonstruck girl of twelve. I imagined myself mistaken by passersby for a scarecrow.

Sometimes I saw myself as a human weed, useless to other people in general and maybe harmful in some weedy way. The notion wasn't entirely unpleasant. Jack Hucklebone: a weed among the well-established money crops of life.

On my way to town with Miss Milky, I crossed over the irrigation ditch my father had fallen into with the stroke that killed him. I pulled over onto the shoulder and switched off the engine. It was a warm, insect-loud day in early June. A spray of grasshoppers clattered over the hood of the truck. June bugs ticked past the windows like little flying clocks. The thirteen-year locusts were back and raising a whirring hell. I was fifteen the last time they came but I didn't remember them arriving in such numbers. I expected more helicopters to come flapping over with special sprays meant just for them, even though they would be around for only a few weeks and the damage they would do is not much more than measurable. But anything that looks like it might have an appetite for a money crop brings down the spraying choppers. I climbed out of the truck and looked up into the bright air. A lone jet, eastbound, too high to see or hear, left its neat chalk line across the top of the sky. The sky itself was hot blue wax, north to south. A fat hammerhead squatted on the west horizon. It looked like a creamy oblong planet that had slipped its orbit and was now endangering the earth.

There's where Daddy died. Up the ditch about fifty yards from here. I found him, buckled, white as paper, half under water. His one good eye, his right (he'd lost the left one thirty years ago when a tractor tire blew up in his face as he was filling it), was above water and wide open, staring at his hand as if it could focus on the thing it gripped. He was holding on to a root. He had big hands, strong, with fingers like thick hardwood dowels, but now they were soft and puffy, like the hands of a giant baby. Water bugs raced against the current toward him. His body blocked the ditch and little eddies swirled around it. The water bugs skated into the eddies and, fighting to hold themselves still in the roiling current, touched his face. They held still long enough to satisfy their curiosity, then slid back into the circular flow as if bemused by the strangeness of dead human flesh.

I started to cry, remembering it, thinking about him in the water, he had been so sure and strong, but then—true to my changed nature—I began to laugh at the memory, for his wide blue eye had had a puzzled cast to it, as if it had never before seen such an oddity as the ordinary root in his forceless hand. It was an expression he never wore in life.

"It was only a weed, Daddy," I said, wiping the tears from my face.

The amazed puzzlement stayed in his eye until I brushed down the lid.

Of course he had been dead beyond all talk and puzzlement. Dead when I found him, dead for hours, bloated dead. And this is how *I've* come to be—blame the spray or don't: the chores don't get done on time, the unplanted fields wait, Mama wanders in her mind, and yet I'll sit in the shade of my truck sipping on Lewis and Clark bourbon, inventing the thoughts of a dead man.

Time bent away from me like a tail-dancing rainbow. It was about to slip the hook. I wasn't trying to hold it. Try to hold it and it gets all the more slippery. Try to let it go and it sticks like a cocklebur to cotton. I was drifting somewhere between the two kinds of not trying: not trying to hold anything, not trying to let anything go.

Then he sat down next to me. The old man.

"You got something for me?" he said.

He was easily the homeliest man I had ever seen. His bald head was bullet-shaped and his lumpy nose was warty as a crookneck squash. His little, close-set eyes sat on either side of that nose like hard black beans. He had shaggy eyebrows that climbed upward in a white and wiry tangle. There was a blue lump in the middle of his forehead the size of a pullet's egg, and his hairy earlobes touched his grimy collar. He was mumbling something, but it could have been the noise of the ditch water as it sluiced through the culvert under the road.

He stank of whiskey and dung, and looked like he'd been sleeping behind barns for weeks. His clothes were rags and he was caked with dirt from fingernail to jaw. His shoes were held together with strips of burlap. He untied some of these strips and took off his shoes. Then he slid his gnarled, corn-crusted feet into the water. His eyes fluttered shut and he let out a hissing moan of pleasure. His toes were long and twisted, the arthritic knuckles painfully bright. They reminded me of the surface roots of a stunted oak that had been trying to grow in hardpan. Though he was only about five feet tall, his feet were huge. Easy size twelves, wide as paddles.

He quit mumbling, cleared his throat, spit. "You got anything for me?" he said.

I handed him my pint. He took it, held it up to the sunlight, looked through the rusty booze as if testing for its quality.

"If it won't do," I said, "I could run down into town and get something a little smoother for you. Maybe you'd like some Canadian Club or some twelve-year-old Scotch. I could run into town and be back in less than an hour. Maybe you'd like me to bring back a couple of fried chickens and a sack of buttered rolls." This was my old self talking, the hothead. But I didn't feel mad at him and was just being mouthy out of habit.

"No need to do that," he said, as if my offer had been made in seriousness. He took a long pull off my pint. "This snake piss is just fine by me, son." He raised the bottle to the sunlight again, squinted through it.

I wandered down the ditch again to the place where Daddy died. There was nothing there to suggest a recent dead man had blocked the current. Everything was as it always was. The water surged, the quick water bugs skated up and down inspecting brown clumps of algae along the banks, underwater weeds waved like slim snakes whose tails had been staked to the mud. I looked for the thistle he'd grabbed on to. I guess he thought that he was going to save himself from drowning by hanging on to its root, not realizing that the killing flood was *inside* his head. But there were many roots along the bank and none of them seemed more special than any other.

Something silver glinted at me. It was a coin. I picked it out of the slime and polished it against my pants. It was a silver dollar, a real one. It could have been his. He carried a few of the old cartwheels around with him for luck. The heft and gleam of the old silver coin choked me up.

I walked back to the old man. He had stuffed his bindle under his head for a pillow and had dozed off. I uncapped the pint and finished it, then flipped it into the weeds. It hit a rock and popped. The old man grunted and his eyes snapped open. He let out a barking snort and his black eyes darted around fiercely, like the eyes of a burrowing animal caught in a daylight trap. Then, remembering where he was, he calmed down.

"You got something for me?" he asked. He pushed himself up to a sitting position. It was a struggle for him.

"Not any more," I said. I sat down next to him. Then, from behind us, a deep groan cut loose. It sounded like siding being pried off a barn with a crow bar. We both turned to look at whatever had complained so mightily.

It was Miss Milky, up in the trailer, venting her misery. I'd forgotten about her. Horseflies were biting her. Black belts of them girdled her teats. Her red eyes peered sadly out at us through the bars. The corners of her eyes were swollen, giving her a Chinese look.

With no warning at all, a snapping hail fell on us. Only it wasn't hail. It was a moving cloud of thirteen-year locusts. They darkened the sky and they covered us. The noise was like static on the radio, miles of static across the bug-peppered sky, static that could drown out all important talk and idle music no matter how powerful the station.

The old man's face was covered with the bugs and he was saying something to me but I couldn't make out what it was. His mouth opened and closed, opened and closed. When it opened he'd have to brush away the locusts from his lips. They were like ordinary grasshoppers, only smaller, and they had big red eyes that seemed to glow with their own hellish light. Then, as fast as they had come, they were gone, scattered back into the fields. A few hopped here and there, but the main cloud had broken up.

I just sat there brushing at the lingering feel of them on my skin and trying to readjust myself to uncluttered air but my ears were still crackling with their racket.

The old man pulled at my sleeve, breaking me out of my daydream or trance. "You got something for me?" he asked.

I felt blue. Worse than blue. Sick. I felt incurable—ridden with the pointlessness of just about everything you could name. The farm struck me as a pointless wonder and I found the idea depressing and fearsome. Pointless bugs lay waiting in the fields for the pointless crops as the pointless days and seasons ran on and on into the pointless forever.

"Shit," I said.

"I'll take that worthless cow off your hands, then," said the old man. "She's done for. All you have to do is look at her."

He didn't seem so old or so wrecked to me now. He was younger and bigger somehow, as if all his clocks had started running backwards, triggered by the locust cloud. He stood up. He looked thick across the shoulders like he'd done hard work all his life and could still do it. He showed me his right hand. It was yellow with hard calluses. His beady black eyes were quick and lively in their shallow sockets. The blue lump on his forehead glinted in the sun. It seemed deliberately polished as if it were an ornament. He took a little silver bell out of his pocket and rang it for no reason at all.

"Let me have her," he said.

"You want Miss Milky?" I asked. I felt weak and child-ish. Maybe I was drunk. My scalp itched and I scratched it hard. He rang his little silver bell again. I wanted to have it but he put it back into his pocket. Then he knelt down and opened his bindle. He took out a paper sack.

I looked inside. It was packed with seeds of some kind. I ran my fingers through them and did not feel foolish. I heard a helicopter putt-putting in the distance. I'll say this in defense of what I did: I knew Miss Milky was done for.

227

Doc Nevers would have told me to shoot her. I don't think she was even good for hamburger. Old cow meat can sometimes make good hamburger but Miss Milky looked wormy and lean. And I wouldn't have trusted her bones for soup. The poison that had wasted her flesh and ruined her udder had probably settled in her marrow.

And so I unloaded my dying cow. He took out his silver bell and tied it to a piece of string. He tied the string around Miss Milky's neck. Then he led her away. She was docile and easy as though this was exactly the way things were supposed to turn out.

My throat was dry. I felt too tired to move. I watched their slow progress down the path that ran along the ditch. They got smaller and smaller until, against a dark hedge of box elders, they disappeared. I strained to see after them, but it was as if the earth had given them refuge, swallowing them into its deep, loamy, composting interior. The only sign that they still existed in the world was the tinkling of the silver bell he had tied around Miss Milky's neck. It was a pure sound, naked on the air.

Then a breeze opened up a gap in the box elders and a long blade of sunlight pierced through them, illuminating and magnifying the old man and his cow, as if the air between us had formed itself into a giant lens. The breeze let up and the box elders shut off the sun again and I couldn't see anything but a dense quiltwork of black and green shadows out of which a raven big as an eagle flapped. It cawed in raucous good humor as it veered over my head.

I went into town anyway, cow or no cow, and hit some bars. I met a girl from the East in the Hobble who thought I was a cowboy and I didn't try to correct her mistaken impression for it proved a free pass to good times.

When I got home Mama had company. She was dressed up in her beet juice gown and her face was powdered white. Her dark lips looked like a wine stain in snow but her clear blue eyes were direct and calm. There was no distraction in them.

"Hi, boy," said the visitor. It was Big Pete Parley. He was wearing a blue suit, new boots, a gray felt Stetson. He had a toothy grin on his fat red face.

I looked at Mama. "What's *he* want?" I asked. Something was wrong. I could feel it but I couldn't see it. It was Mama, the way she had composed herself maybe, or the look in her eyes, or her whitened skin. Maybe she had gone all the way insane. She went over to Parley and sat next to him on the davenport. She had slit her gown and it fell away from her thigh, revealing the veiny flesh.

"We're going to be married," she said. "Pete's tired of being a widower. He wants a warm bed."

As if to confirm it was no fantasy dreamed up by her senile mind, Big Pete slid his hand into the slit dress and squeezed her thigh. He clicked his teeth and winked at me.

"Pete knows how to run a farm," said Mama. "And you do not, Jackie." She didn't intend for it to sound mean or critical. It was just a statement of the way things were. I couldn't argue with her.

I went into the kitchen. Mama followed me in. I opened

a beer. "I don't mean to hurt your feelings, Jackie," she said.

"He's scheming to get our land," I said. "He owns half the county, but that isn't enough."

"No," she said. "I'm the one who's scheming. I'm scheming for my boy who does not grasp the rudiments of the world."

I had the sack of seeds with me. I realized that I'd been rattling them nervously.

"What do you have there?" she asked, narrowing her eyes.

"Seeds," I said.

"Seeds? What seeds? Who gave you seeds? Where did you get them?"

I thought it best not to mention where I'd gotten them. "Big Pete Parley doesn't want to marry *you*," I said. It was a mean thing to say and I wanted to say it.

Mama sighed. "It doesn't matter what he wants, Jack. I'm dead anyway." She took the bag of seeds from me, picked some up, squinted at them.

"What is that supposed to mean?" I said, sarcastically.

She went to the window above the sink and stared out into the dark. Under the folds of her evening gown I could see the ruined shape of her old body. "Dead, Jack," she said. "I've been dead for a while now. Maybe you didn't notice."

"No," I said. "I didn't."

"Well, you should have. I went to sleep shortly after

your Daddy died and I had a dream. The dream got stronger and stronger as it went on until it was as vivid as real life itself. More vivid. When I woke up I knew that I had died. I also knew that nothing in the world would ever be as real to me as that dream."

I almost asked her what the dream was about but I didn't, out of meanness. In the living room Big Pete Parley was whistling impatiently. The davenport was squeaking under his nervous weight.

"So you see, Jackie," said Mama. "It doesn't matter if I marry Pete Parley or what his motives are in the matter. You are all that counts now. He will ensure your success in the world."

"I don't want to be a success, Mama," I said.

"Well, you have no choice. You cannot gainsay the dead."

She opened the window over the kitchen sink and dumped out the sack of seeds. Then Big Pete Parley came into the kitchen. "Let's go for a walk," he said. "It's too blame hot in this house."

They left by the kitchen door. I watched them walk across the yard and into the dark, unplanted field. Big Pete had his arm around Mama's shoulder. I wondered if he knew, or cared, that he was marrying a dead woman. Light from the half-moon painted their silhouettes for a while. Then the dark field absorbed them.

I went to bed and slept for what might have been days.

In my long sleep I had a dream. I was canoeing down a whitewater river that ran sharply uphill. The farther up I got, the rougher the water became. Finally, I had to beach the canoe. I proceeded on foot until I came to a large gray house that had been built in a wilderness forest. The house was empty and quiet. I went in. It was clean and beautifully furnished. Nobody was home. I called out a few times before I understood that silence was a rule. I went from room to room, going deeper and deeper toward some dark interior place. I understood that I was involved in a search. The longer I searched, the more vivid the dream became.

When I woke up I was stiff and weak. Mama wasn't in the house. I made a pot of coffee and took a cup outside. Under the kitchen window there was a patch of green shoots that had not been there before. "You got something for me?" I said.

A week later that patch of green shoots had grown and spread. They were weeds. The worst kind of weeds I had ever seen. Thick, spiny weeds with broad green leaves tough as leather. They rolled away from the house, out across the field, in a viny carpet. Mean, deep-rooted weeds, too mean to uproot by hand. When I tried, I came away with a palm full of cuts.

In another week they were tall as corn. They were fast growers and I could not see where they ended. They covered everything in sight. A smothering blanket of deep green sucked the life out of every other growing thing.

They crossed fences, irrigation ditches, and when they reached the trees of a windbreak, they became ropy crawlers that wrapped themselves around trunks and limbs.

When they reached the Parley farm, over which my dead mother now presided, they were attacked by squadrons of helicopters which drenched them in poisons, the best poisons chemical science knew how to brew. But the poisons only seemed to make the weeds grow faster, and after a spraying the new growths were tougher, thornier, and more determined than ever to dominate the land.

Some of the weeds sent up long woody stalks. On top of these stalks were heavy seedpods, fat as melons. The strong stalks pushed the pods high into the air.

The day the pods cracked a heavy wind came up. The wind raised black clouds of seed in grainy spirals that reached the top of the sky, then scattered them, far and wide, across the entire nation.

KENT MEYERS

THE HEART OF THE SKY

It surprised even me when Lennis Wagner filled in his tile intake and let the slough he'd drained re-form. To go out with a shovel and sledgehammer and smash the tile intake, after spending all that money putting it in and getting good crops off the reclaimed land, and to fill the intake up with dirt—at first I didn't believe it, quite, even though Lennis himself told me he'd done it. Like everyone else, I waited for the proof. It took two years to come—cattails reasserting themselves, and finally the red-winged and yellow-headed blackbirds waving on the ends of reeds chirruping, and the sounds of frogs rolling across the fields clear to my place in the evenings.

I've been good friends with Lennis since high school, and we still work together, but it took him a long time to tell me what had happened—chinks of talk filling in the spaces between work. It was obvious enough to everyone when Adrian became pregnant, but no one ever thought to connect that to Lennis taking a hammer to his tile.

He and Mary were sitting in their living room one evening before going to bed. Lennis has even told me what he was reading—a *Successful Farming* magazine—and Mary was doing a crossword puzzle, when Adrian came downstairs. Lennis glanced up from his magazine and saw the expression on her face, and, he says, knew right then what she was going to say. He was on his feet and moving toward her before she'd finished with, 'Dad. Mom. I have to talk to you.'

Adrian used to hover around her father while he worked, and he'd stop to answer her questions, put up with her attempts to help. Mary was more demanding, less close to her daughter. Small enough, even healthy, differences, I suppose—differences a family can ignore. But crises magnify such differences. By the time Adrian spoke her next words, her father had her in his arms, while Mary was still sitting in her chair.

It's not hard to see how things can set and harden in an instant. Years of a family living within its tensions carefully, keeping them from congealing, flexible, like moving in molasses—and then, like that, everything is set.

There was Mary, watching.

'You're pregnant.' She repeated Adrian's words. A statement. With accusation inside it. The only available option, really, with Lennis having preempted sympathy and understanding. And stared at her husband and daughter with a face collapsed like a balloon losing air.

She couldn't see what Lennis himself felt. He told me he

felt like throwing Adrian from him. "My own daughter, Charlie," he said. "You know what that feels like? I wanted to throw her down and then find the punk she met at the damn canning factory and pound him. That's what I really wanted to do."

But he's not the kind of man to let his emotions get out of control. He kept his arms around Adrian. Told himself what's done is done.

Of course Mary couldn't see that. She looked at Adrian held in her father's arms and said dryly, 'Well, Adrian, I am disappointed. I thought you knew better.'

Adrian had been sobbing, but at her mother's words she stopped. She brought her face up from her father's chest. 'I'm sorry, Mom.'

'But you love him. And that's going to make everything all right.'

So much is missing here. So much of what might have been said.

Adrian struggled to free herself from Lennis's arms. To face her mother. Lennis had to let her go.

But even the wrong thing said is something said. A risk. A commitment to something. Lennis is an awfully good friend, but I wonder: why'd he say nothing? Why listen through all this?

'Mom,' Adrian said. Addressing only her mother. The various ways families shut each other out. 'I never wanted—'

Mary interrupted. 'So you're making me a grandmother. Do you know how old that makes me feel?'

For a second Adrian stared at her mother. Then flung herself away. Lennis reached for her again, but she ducked around him, her hair swinging against her face. She fled up the stairs sobbing. His face stung as if her hair had ripped it off the bones.

He couldn't face Mary. He spoke without looking at her. 'You didn't even touch her.'

'And you coddled her,' Mary replied bleakly. 'Nothing she does ever bothers you, does it?'

He walked away from her without another word.

When a family begins to resemble a church service, something's gone awry. Lennis didn't tell me all this until much later, but I could tell something was wrong. Too much politeness. "Yeah," I said when he finally began to talk about it. "I knew something was wrong. Couldn't say anything, but all those pleases and thank-yous whenever we worked together and I ate lunch with you. A few too many, I thought."

We were stacking straw. Lennis laughed and leaned against the stack. "We were that polite?"

"You were."

But they never talked about what needed talking about. I can't imagine what Adrian must have been going through. Poor girl. Right when she most needs her parents, they're not speaking—not to her or to each other. Except for please and thank you.

Lennis escaped into harvest. Soybeans were ready, a frost having dried them out, and he combined with a vengeance. A good excuse—as he himself said later—to stay away from the house. Just keep going. Watch the beans fall. Watch the tank fill up. Nothing like the momentum of a combine. Damn near a narcotic.

Then the old slough entered the picture. Through the dust rising off the circling reel one day, Lennis noticed a flash of white among the dried-out vines. As the combine sliced toward it, he made out the narrow neck and half-raised wings of a Canada goose. No one I know ever thrilled more to the sound of geese's honking coming down from the sky. In high school, once I was riding with him when he heard geese, and he stuck his head out the window looking for the flock and drove the car right into the road ditch. He hit a field approach and bounced back onto the road. I was screaming at him, seeing that approach looming, but he never heard me. Never saw. Kept his head in the wind, his eyes on the sky. Ended up mildly surprised at the rough ride. When we were back on the road, asked me what'd happened.

'Oh,' he said when I told him. Then: 'Awful big flock. Two hundred, I bet.'

So the sight of a Canada goose in his soybean field should have at least made him curious. But he was still numb from the rift Adrian's announcement had opened in the family. He kept his eyes on the sickle. He was almost on top of the bird before he realized it wasn't going to lift from the field. He jerked back on the hydrostatics, and the combine rocked to a halt, wailing as the threshing drum emptied. Lennis looked down from the dusty dials. The goose stretched its neck toward the flickering sickle. Its small, pointed tongue pulsed. Lennis waited for it to realize the enormity of the machine—the thirty-foot header, the cab looming like a cliff.

But the goose gave no ground.

Lennis had his hand on the hydrostatics. He felt nothing. If he pushed the lever, there would be a lurch, a small drop in RPMs. Then the field would lie flat before him again. On the return round he might find a few feathers. A red stain in the stubble. But most likely not. Most likely just dust.

But the wait. It was just enough, he told me, to take him out of the harvest. To remember. How Adrian's hair had stung his face. "It's a funny thing," is the way he put it to me, "but as long as I was combining, I was able to forget it, pretty much. Adrian. Mary. Just go out and watch the beans fall. Watch the tank fill. But when that goose stopped me, I felt it all over again. Like it'd been waiting outside me for a chance to step back in. Where it really belonged. Her hair was like whips, Charlie. Whips, and then silence. And me and Mary with nothing good to say."

239

He disengaged everything, let the combine idle. Beyond the goose, an orange flag marked the tile intake. He was in the middle of the old slough. His father had refused to drain it. Lennis, more modern, seeing profit, had tiled it as soon as the old man died. No big deal. Everybody tiled. With taxes and all, it's hard to afford not to. Still, it's too bad. Geese and ducks used to descend like the sky itself in the fall. Bring the sky right down with them, like they were stitching it to the earth. Into all the sloughs this country contained. Everything turned wild in the fall. Lennis and I grew up in that—sloughs all over for exploring. And not just geese. Muskrats. Frogs. Herons. Egrets. Fox. Birds of all kinds. Most of that's gone now. When Lennis tiled his slough, that was about the last one around, and the geese just go on over now. High up. Sometimes we don't see them at all. And most of the other animals, too—replaced by emptiness. Crops, sure. But I look around sometimes and don't wonder why kids now prefer Nintendo. This land's more contained than the screen is.

On the other hand, Lennis let his slough come back, and even I tell him he's crazy. And most people actually believe it.

He climbed down the ladder and trudged around the platform. The orange flag marking the tile intake snapped in the breeze.

The bird half-raised its wings, threatening.

'Gwan,' Lennis said, waving his arms. 'Outta here!'

He stepped toward it.

The bird attacked.

Lennis jumped back, nearly tripping in the soybeans. "You shoulda seen it, Charlie," he told me. "Came at me faster'n I could believe. Wings back, hunched. Hissing. Scared the crap out of me."

'Well, I'll be damned,' he muttered when he'd recovered and the goose had retreated into the soybeans. He examined the bird for signs of injury, but it had nothing of the listless, droopy look of a sick animal. He went at it again, waving his arms and yelling, but the goose just turned on him like it had before, forcing him to retreat. He'd never seen anything like it.

Dust hazed the sun. It mixed with the smell of diesel exhaust and blew away. The wind dropped. Lennis, confounded by the goose, looked across the field. Saw his house. Squatting on the land. Looking alone, isolated. Plunked down. He thought of Mary and Adrian inside it. Saying nothing.

"The craziest thing," he told me, "but when the wind stopped out there, it seemed that the stillness was all pouring out of the house. Don't laugh now, Charlie. Stillness just pouring out. And Adrian there. My daughter. I was combining soybeans, right? Had to be done. But I swear, Charlie, when I thought of her in that house like that, I wondered what the hell I was doing in the field."

Still, the goose was in the row. Even if he wanted to be with Adrian, he had to finish the round. No rule about it, but no farmer'd leave a round unfinished. He turned his attention back to the bird, windmilled his arms, yelled. The goose refused to move. Kept attacking. Lennis had to leap rows to avoid it. Sweat poured down his face, made furrows in the dust on his forearms.

And all for nothing. The bird looked healthy. There couldn't possibly be a nest here. It just plain refused to fly.

Damn animal.

He'd done enough. Tried. Taken the time to do the good thing. He couldn't wait here forever.

"I said screw it," he told me. "That's where I was at. Just screw the bird. Get on with things. If it thought it owned the field, all right."

He turned his back and climbed to the cab. The goose sank into the soybean vines. Lennis looked down at it. Then engaged the machinery. Belts squealed. The reel swept around. The judder and jar of the sickle came up through the metal. Lennis pulled down the throttle. The threshing drum moaned, rose to a pitch, howled. Soybean dust and dirt flew off the painted side of the combine and blew out the back. Obscured the lowering sun.

Lennis looked down once more.

The bird didn't move. Stupid. Stubborn.

All right. Lennis engaged the hydrostatics. The engine bellowed, and the combine floated through the soybeans, devouring them.

The goose attacked. Ran right toward the sickle.

But Lennis saw, suddenly, why it wouldn't fly.

He jerked back on the hydrostatics so hard he lost his balance as the machine stopped. He slipped, knocked the lever forward again, the combine jerking, before he finally managed to stop it. Without even bothering to disengage the machinery, Lennis yanked the fuel cutoff. Everything fell to a strange, unnatural silence. When he slipped, Lennis lost sight of the bird. He had his eyes shut. The last thing he'd seen had been the bird and sickle, inches apart, rushing at each other.

He didn't want to look. "From above it, I saw the problem," he told me. "Its wings were catching on the vines. You know how soybean vines get. Hell. It's been trying to fly all the time. Raising its wings halfway, and me thinking it was threatening. All it was trying to do was get them over the vines so it could get out of there. Couldn't be done. Once it got into that row, it was trapped.

"I just put my head on the steering wheel with my eyes shut," he said. "Couldn't even look at what I'd done, Charlie."

And then—sound. He lifted his head. In wonder. There, standing inches from the header, its neck stretched to the sky, the goose was honking. Pouring out wildness. Muted through the glass, it sounded to Lennis as if it came from high clouds. Dropping down. A sound he hadn't heard in years. A sound he'd once driven into a road ditch trying to find.

He hadn't counted on the wild reflexes of the goose. When he slipped, it must have turned and fled the machine, its bluff called. Lennis listened to it, and his eyes filled. He told me that, and it's not an easy thing for a man to say.

"My love for the birds came back," he said. "Do you remember it, Charlie? How we loved them? We didn't just like them. We loved them. God, I'd forgotten. Just let myself forget. And not just the geese. Everything. Frogs, snakes, birds' nests, odd-shaped sticks. You remember, don't you?"

We were picking up rocks together when he told me this part of it. He wanted me to remember. I could tell. It was important to him. We leaned against the bale rack together, where we had a pile of rocks tumbled. I stared across his field. The slough he'd let come back was two hundred yards away. A mirror. A patch of sky. Framed by reeds. Set in the black earth.

"Yeah," I said. "I remember."

And I did. I remembered hiding in those reeds with him, just a couple of kids, watching the geese come down. Pour down. Like rain. Or snow. Drifting down to fill the slough. And us inside it all. Right there, with them. Inside the flock. Whispering.

Lennis nodded. Satisfied. "Yeah," he said. "Well, once I remembered that, I remembered how much I loved Adrian. Not just like I wanted her to be. But right now. As she was. And Mary, too. Like hunting, Charlie. How many times did we find something different than what were looking for?"

"That's a question," I said. "But hell. These rocks aren't picking themselves up."

So he started the combine again and backed it away from the goose. Shut the machine off, descended the ladder again. This time he could see the goose's wings catch in the brittle vines arching over the narrow rows, even hear the feathers scrape.

Lennis squatted down and regarded the bird for a while. Then stood. And ran.

Right at it.

The goose flared, hissing, its wings hunching again, its neck coming forward snakelike. But Lennis ran right into it. Scooped it up like a football. His feet caught in the vines as he grabbed the bird, and he stumbled. The goose's freed wings beat the air around Lennis, beat his head and ears. His face was caught in the vacuum and thrust of the wings, his ears full of their whistle and throw. One white confusion of hard air and bone, coming so fast he couldn't feel the blows. Pulling the goose away from him.

A good friend. It's all right to envy him this.

His whole purpose was to free the goose, but now that he held it, something in him resisted letting go. He hauled the bird in close and turned his head against its breast. His right ear pressed into the soft down. Then the tangle of soybeans clutched his feet. He fell. Throwing the goose up and away as he went down. But he'd heard for a moment an eternal thing. The goose's heartbeat, wild and brilliant, under the feathers. "The heart of the sky, Charlie," he said. "It was."

Then the ground rose up and jarred his wingless body. He hit and rolled and saw the bird tumble in the air. Straighten. Saw its wings cover the sky, come down together over him. He felt the backwash of air against his face. The goose lifted itself away from him as he lay on his back. It grew smaller. Smaller. The sky was a blue emptiness, with wind.

By the time he'd done chores, washed, and eaten, Mary was already in bed, reading. Avoiding talk. But he went in to her. He sat on the edge of the bed until she looked up from her book.

'How was your day?' he asked her.

'Fine.'

'I didn't get the beans finished.'

'Oh.'

'I ran into some trouble.'

She didn't respond. Went back to her book.

'How's Adrian?'

'She's fine.'

'That's nowhere near true, is it, Mary?' he said.

Her eyes swept the page.

'She's pregnant. Seventeen and pregnant, Mary. That's sure not fine. And we haven't even talked about it.'

Mary went completely still. "Completely still," he told me. "I reached out and touched her hair. And said, 'You know, Mary, some of this is turning gray.' "

"Just the kind of thing to endear a man to his wife," I said.

At which he smiled.

Mary's breath caught. Like a dry leaf swept against a wall by wind. She let her book drop into her lap.

'Hell, Mary,' he went on. 'You're old enough to be a grandmother. And you know what? That's not her fault.'

'Damn you,' she whispered.

'Sometimes we're all damn fools, Mary. I know you love her. I do too. I love you, Mary. Go to her, will you? It's you she needs right now.'

Mary wept. Gripped his hand and wept.

They listened to their daughter moving in her room upstairs. Lennis looked out the window, a blank darkness beyond which the wind blew across the fields.

'That trouble I had,' he said. 'It was a Canada goose. It'd come down where that slough used to be. Like it knew it was supposed to be there. It couldn't get back up. Got between the rows and couldn't spread its wings.'

'What'd you do?'

'Tried to chase it up. It just attacked me.'

'So what'd you do?'

We were crouched in cattails when he got around to telling me this part of it. We'd heard high geese that morning, each of us on our separate farms, and I knew when my wife yelled at me that Lennis was on the phone what he'd be saying: "You must have chores done by now. Maybe we can see some set their wings."

"So what'd you tell her, then?" I asked.

"Pretty odd. For some reason, I didn't know what to say all of a sudden."

"Why not? Seems pretty clear to me."

"I don't know. Strange. Something in me just went private. And I couldn't tell her. I was afraid I'd lose it, maybe. Its heart. The sky's. That make any sense?"

"Probably not," I said.

"And Mary and I were as close right then as we'd maybe ever been."

"But you told me, Lennis."

"Yeah. Figure that out."

"So what'd you tell her?"

"I ran it through."

"You told her you ran it through the combine?"

He nodded. "In a way, I did, too. Would have. The bird just managed to escape first."

Mary was shocked.

'You ran it through the combine?' Her voice, he says, was thin as paper.

'It wouldn't move,' he said. 'I couldn't make it move.'

"You think that was the best thing to tell her?" I asked.

"I don't know. It's what I told her. In some ways it doesn't matter. I just wanted Adrian okay. And what the hell was that goose doing there anyway? You never see a single goose. It was like it was waiting for me. You able to explain that?"

"No. All I know is, you're losing a lot of money on this slough."

"Suppose I am."

"A lot of people think you're crazy. You know that?"

We heard a sound like dogs barking, far away in the sky. But in a moment our ears adjusted, and it wasn't barking at all. It was the clear bugle honk of geese.

"You can't afford to farm this way. You know that?"

But he was looking at the sky.

ABOUT THE AUTHORS

DIANE ACKERMAN, a poet and nature writer, is the author of more than a dozen books, including *A Natural History of the Senses, The Moon by Whale Light, A Slender Thread,* and *Deep Play.* The recipient of numerous awards and a frequent contributor to *National Geographic* and *The New York Times,* Ackerman also writes children's books, which include *Bats: Shadows in the Night.* Ackerman has taught at various universities and lives with her husband, the writer Paul West, in Ithaca, New York.

MARGARET ATWOOD, a resident of Toronto, is the author of more than twenty-five books, including the brilliant and unique short story collections *Wilderness Tips* and *Good Bones and Simple Murders,* many volumes of poetry and nonfiction, and such acclaimed and indelible novels as *Life Before Man, The Handmaid's Tale, Cat's Eye, The Robber Bride,* and *Alias Grace.*

RICK BASS, a prominent voice in the environmental movement, lives in Montana's Yaak Valley and writes about wilderness and wildness in both his celebrated nonfiction, which includes books about wolves and grizzlies and the

251

essay collection *The Book of Yaak*, and his stellar fiction, which ranges from his novel *Where the Sea Used to Be* to the short fiction collections *The Sky, the Stars, the Wilderness* and *In the Loyal Mountains.*

RICK DEMARINIS is the author of six novels, including *The Year of the Zinc Penny,* which was chosen as a *New York Times* Notable Book in 1989. His remarkable, unsettling, original stories, which have appeared in *Harper's, Antaeus,* and *Story,* among others, have been collected in *Borrowed Hearts: New and Selected Stories.* DeMarinis teaches creative writing at the University of Texas, El Paso.

E. L. DOCTOROW is one of the most distinguished and influential writers of our times, as well as an eloquent spokesman for human rights. The author of such seminal works as *The Book of Daniel, Ragtime, Lives of the Poets, World's Fair, The Waterworks,* and *City of God,* Doctorow has garnered the National Book Critics Circle Award twice, the National Book Award, the PEN/Faulkner Award, the William Dean Howells Medal of the American Academy of Arts and Letters, and the presidentially conferred National Humanities Medal. Doctorow continues to live and write in his hometown of New York City.

PERCIVAL EVERETT is one of America's most imaginative writers, taking on a new voice and experimenting with form in each work of fiction. He has written twelve books, including the short story collection *Big Picture* and the novels *Watershed, Frenzy,* and *Glyph.* Everett lives on a farm in Southern California with his wife and teaches at the University of Southern California.

TESS GALLAGHER is best known as a poet, but she is also the author of two wild-at-heart short story collections, *The Lover of Horses and Other Stories* and *At the Owl Woman Saloon,* as well as essay collections and screenplays cowritten with her late husband, Raymond Carver. Gallagher teaches at Whitman College in Walla Walla, Washington, and lives in Sky House in Port Angeles, Washington.

LINDA HOGAN, a renowned Chickasaw poet, short story writer, novelist, and essayist, lives and writes in Colorado. Wilderness is at the heart of her books, including *Mean Spirit,* which received the Oklahoma Book Award and the Mountains and Plains Booksellers Award; the American Book Award–winning poetry collection *Seeking Through the Sun*; the nonfiction work *Dwellings: Reflections on the Natural World*; and the mystical novels *Solar Storms* and *Power.*

BARRY LOPEZ's name has been synonymous with nature writing ever since he won the National Book Award for *Arctic Dreams.* The author, too, of such environmentally sensitive nonfiction works as *Of Wolves and Men* and *About This Life: Journeys on the Threshold of Memory*, Lopez has also written wilderness fiction, including *Field Notes, Lessons from the Wolverine*, and *River Notes*. A contributing editor at *Harper's*, Lopez lives in western Oregon.

PAULINE MELVILLE, currently a Londoner, grew up in Guyana, and her incisive and inventive fiction reflects her cosmopolitanism. Her first book, the short story collection *Shape-Shifter*, was awarded the *Guardian* Fiction Prize. *The Ventriloquist's Tale* won the Whitbread First Novel Award, and her second book of stories, *The Migration of Ghosts*, has earned widespread critical acclaim.

KENT MEYERS is the author of an essay collection, *The Witness of Combines*, and two works of soulful fiction set in the small farming town of Cloten, Minnesota: the novel *The River Warren* and the radiant, surprising, and profoundly moving short story collection *Light in the Crossing*. He lives in Spearfish, South Dakota.

LORRIE MOORE dazzles readers with her wit and tenderness in novels and short story collections, which include *Who Will Run the Frog Hospital?*, *Self-Help*, and *Birds of America*. Her stylistically pristine, heartfelt, humorous, and vital work has appeared in *The New Yorker, The Best*

American Short Stories, and *Prize Stories: The O. Henry Awards.* Moore is a professor of English at the University of Wisconsin, Madison.

CHRIS OFFUTT galvanized the literary community with his debut story collection, *Kentucky Straight.* Named one of *Granta*'s twenty Best Young American Fiction Writers, he has received awards from the Guggenheim Foundation, the American Academy of Arts and Letters, and the Whiting Foundation. He is also the author of *The Same River Twice, The Good Brother,* and the stunning *Out of the Woods.*

SIMON J. ORTIZ, a native of Acoma Pueblo in New Mexico, is a poet, fiction writer, essayist, and storyteller. His books include *Speaking for the Generations, The People Shall Continue,* and *Men on the Moon.* Ortiz has received awards from the National Endowment for the Arts and the Lila Wallace–Reader's Digest Fund, a "Returning the Gift" Lifetime Achievement Award, and a New Mexico Humanities Council Humanitarian Award. He lives in Tucson, Arizona.

FRANCINE PROSE is the author of ten acclaimed novels, including *Hunters and Gatherers, Bigfoot Dreams, Household Saints,* and *Blue Angel,* as well as short story collections, including *The Peaceable Kingdom.* Prose's acute short stories have appeared in *The New Yorker,* the *Atlantic,* *GQ,* and the *Paris Review,* and her literary criticism is widely published. Prose teaches at the New School and is a fellow at the New York Public Library's Center for Scholars and Writers.

ACKNOWLEDGMENTS

Anthologies are the fruits of avid and sustained reading, a habit of mine that has been given structure and purpose by my colleagues at *Booklist* and the American Library Association, to whom I will always be grateful. I also thank Bart Schneider, Elizabeth Taylor, Carolyn Alessio, Melanie Kroupa, and all the other generous editors who have helped me turn reading into writing. In addition, I must express boundless gratitude for family and friends who encourage and accept with good grace my book-madness.

ABOUT THE EDITOR

DONNA SEAMAN is an editor for *Booklist*, and her reviews and essays have also appeared in the *Chicago Tribune*, the *Boston Review*, the *Los Angeles Times*, and the *Ruminator Review* (formerly the *Hungry Mind Review*). Seaman lives in Chicago, where she hosts "Open Books," a radio show about writers and writing.